FINAL EXAM

FINAL EXAM

LOU PUGLIESE

Final Exam

This is a work of fiction. Names, characters, businesses, places, events, locales, and incidents are either the products of the author's imagination or used in a fictitious manner. Any resemblance to actual persons, living or dead, or actual events is purely coincidental.

Library of Congress Control Number 2025900612

ISBN 979-8-9900726-3-3 (hardcover)
ISBN 979-8-9900726-5-7 (paperback)
ISBN 979-8-9900726-4-0 (e-book)

Book Cover by Chris Holmes
Interior Design by Autumn Skye
Editing by Jennifer Ellen Cook

First edition 2025

FOREWORD

Many thanks to those of you joining me in my latest fiction publication. I'm whelmed by the feedback for *Blame it on the Moon*. Many of you expressed a desire to see more of the characters from that book in other publications. People especially liked Don Weston and Vicki. I'm happy to follow your suggestions.

In *Blame it on the Moon*, Don Weston refers to some serious police activity that occurred at Churchville University the year before he met Richard Craft. This is that story.

UNDER COVER OF DARKNESS

On a moonless night, a figure in dark clothing walked down a quiet street and disappeared as it blended into a thick hedge along one of the houses. This was the home of Dr. Isabel Helms, Churchville University provost, a rental cottage in an old neighborhood of large lots that were parceled out almost a century ago from Mennonite farms. It was just a mile from the Churchville University campus, a short drive or brisk walk for Isabel, depending on the weather and her mood.

The surrounding homes were also simple. Generations of Mennonite kin were well-settled in that area. They were great neighbors, always friendly and ready to help with homeowner chores. They'd also accept help gladly and graciously with their own larger tasks. It was the community way. Aside from that, they were unseen, early to bed and early to rise, and deeply private in their devotions. It fit Isabel's private nature, and she loved it there.

Isabel's house was empty that weekend, not an unusual state. The shadowy visitor entered the back kitchen door undetected. There were no Ring doorbells or security cameras to record an intruder's appearance, or disappearance. The back door was unlocked, not surprising for life in the small town.

Inside, the trespasser walked silently through the rooms. The kitchen led to the great room, divided by furniture into a living room, a library nook, and an office space. Wary of even using a flashlight, the unfamiliar house was a trip-and-fall hazard everywhere. "Damn it. almost took me down there" the trespasser spoke to the unseen ottoman.

Adjusting to the darkness, off the great room, two open doors revealed an antique bath, complete with a clawfoot tub, and a bedroom of reasonable size, tastefully decorated in a more modern theme of comfort. "Cozy."

The stranger sifted through the closet and drawers of the bedroom, finding only the usual and expected professional wear and underthings. There was a vibrator in the nightstand, but that was hardly an alarming discovery in the personal items of a single lady. The shadow then investigated the desktop computer and an iPad that was on a charger in the reading space of the great room. The desktop had a Microsoft platform with a docking station for her business laptop, connected to the university system as a virtual, off-campus university workspace. After a quick look, it was determined to be all business. No need to dwell on that piece of equipment, especially since it gave off a glow that might be noticed if someone passed by the house.

The iPad was her personal device. Sitting on the floor in a dark corner, the iPad surrendered her financial files and passwords. Isabel's finances were quite healthy in savings and investment.

"Smart girl," said the intruder to the empty room. "If you were as savvy in your computer skills as you are in your investments, someone would have had to work much harder to know that."

The easiest access was her recent search history. She was not a dark web cruiser. The figure looked through the browsing history: "Boring, boring, boring. . . Oh wait, what do we have here?" Isabel's visits to conventional websites were expected. This one was not. Xnorml.com was an unsecured, relatively porous site where users of various sexual lifestyle interests could meet.

"And a dirty, dirty girl," muttered the hacker after a quick review.

A knowledgeable user would have known to enlist a VPN and take additional personal security steps before engaging there. Isabel had simply found the site through her iPad search. She was so professional and buttoned up in her public life but, unfortunately, not well-schooled in internet security.

Isabel's activity on Xnorml left her IP address exposed, inviting any interested source of ill will to stalk her further online, eventually piecing together her real identity and residence. Her messaging box indicated an affinity for anonymous encounters of a nature that might be less than respectful for a university provost. "Very pleased to meet you in cyberspace, Ms. Unicorn, and your many pen pals 'bondingwithbondgae', 'submittedcommitted'. and the like."

With this hands-on access to her actual device, a vessel of evil now had all the information needed to search further from their own computer, even cruising with Isabel's identity if chosen. The trespasser hadn't known what to look for when entering Isabel's cottage, but plenty was now found. There was no need to bother looking in the detached garage. "Thanks for your memories, we'll be talking soon," said Isabel's stalker upon exiting. Everything inside and out was left as found, with no sign that a visitor had visited.

Less than twenty minutes from passing the hedgerow, the dark-clad figure was gone.

ONE YEAR AGO

What Cops Do for Fun

Darell Metz was sitting in a rocking chair on the front porch when Don Weston arrived home. Darell was smoking a cigar and drinking a beer. He greeted Don with, "I hope you don't mind that I broke in and raided the fridge and the humidor. You have shitty home security for a cop." Don Weston was the chief of police at Churchville University. He sported a Tom Selleck mustache and stood six-foot-five. He carried a few extra pounds reminiscent of a football lineman. Still, he also wore a great smile, offering a welcoming rather than imposing presence. By contrast, Darell was about five-foot-eight. He had lightly unruly hair and an expressive face equally comfortable with a pensive or amused look.

"Just enough to keep the honest people honest. Always good to see you, my dishonest friend," Don said, shaking Darrel's hand and pulling him in for a bear hug. "How are things going down there in Arlington?"

Darell was a longtime veteran of the Arlington County, Virginia Police Department, a suburb of Washington DC. He and Don first met years ago. They hit it off right from the start and had stayed in touch since.

Darell took a deep breath, settling back into the oversized rocker on Don's wraparound porch. "The county is just coming off an election year. Fortunately, no changes in the department, but the politicians like to scare the residents with criminal conspiracies of illegal aliens and human trafficking these days, so it's been a political football game with no winners. I'd call it a tie. It's just good to have it behind us and get back to whatever normal is. How are things going in your sleepy world?"

"A little less than sleepy and quite political here as well. I've already written my letter of resignation based on current conditions. I may hold it to see what happens with a new development. We're about to do some research on a couple of prospective employees, one potential provost and one that would be the third president Churchville has had in less than a year."

"We, kemosabe?"

"Si, Tonto. You can earn yourself a nice dinner for your labor. Between the two of us, we can likely tackle the main portion of this in a couple of hours."

"Well, a Don Weston hosted dinner is always an event worth working for."

They went through their vetting research over dinner.

From Don's reference calls, Isabel Helms was an easy one and the perfect candidate in all ways, with no question. She had spent her entire academic career at Addison University with nothing but accolades. It might be worth hiring Olson just to get her here.

Harold Olson was a little deeper dive. He was known as a tall, good-looking man of enormous personal certainty and ego. That could have raised a little flag, but Churchville needed someone with confidence to get the ship back in the right direction. Olson seemed to be respected. He had been with several institutions previously, and all gave him glowing reviews on paper as he moved on to seemingly higher pursuits.

Don Weston looked at that movement carefully in the vetting process. That's also the higher academic way of quiet separation. Don found Harold Olson's academic and administrative credentials to be exceptional. He also found hints of things unspoken. This he shared with Darell.

"The reference from Olson's most recent tenure was exactly what I hoped to find since George Hunt, who is heading the search committee, likes this guy as a fit. The HR folks at Addison were open and chatty about how exceptional an administrator he's been. They were sorry to be losing him but excited and supportive of his promotion to university president. His previous references, not so much. They were somewhat tight-lipped on Olson, saying they could only confirm his time of employment. In my cop sense, I tend to put that in the bucket of 'let's just say we parted ways to avoid scandal.' Everything else checks out grandly, so I guess I'll just have to accept that as my bias and stay alert. Did you come up with anything interesting?"

"I did. This one also goes in the cop sense suspicion bucket with no real reason to question it. Olson's wife, Elly, had a 3:00 a.m. traffic stop last year in a questionable Cleveland neighborhood. The reason for the stop was two females in a place and time that might have put them at some risk. The passenger was Isabel Helms. They told the officer they had been traveling all day coming back from a vacation weekend, and they had lost their way to end up where he found them. Nothing suspicious, so he escorted them out of danger and sent them on their way."

"Girls' night out?" suggested Don.

"Who knows? But it would seem to indicate a personal relationship with Isabel and at least one of the Olsons."

"Duly noted," said Don. "Likely just more cop sense bias but one more nagging hint just the same. Dessert's here. We can check their published footprint back at the house."

Home again in the big rockers with fresh beverages and cigars, Don commented wistfully, "It certainly is a nice evening for enjoying the clean country air."

"Very true, Don. There's nothing like the wafting scent of freshly manured fields to stimulate the senses."

They mined the research on social media and newspaper accounts for Harold and Isabel. The public presence was well-disciplined for both. Don had some personal home life questions, but with no absolute proof, those would be only suspicion and not a showstopper for Harold Olson to be the next president of Churchville University.

After a legendary Don Weston breakfast feast the next morning, Darell headed back south.

Harold Olson would be coming to Churchville. The hints were packed away, hopefully forever. In time the truth would turn out to be much more interesting than the hints.

HAROLD AND GEORGE

Upon settling in Churchville, Harold Olson sought the counsel of the head of his search team, prominent local attorney George Hunt, who had also been Churchville's president two administrations before. Dr. Hunt arrived at Harold's office with Don Weston in tow. George embodied the perfect Southern gentleman, always impeccably dressed in a light-colored suit. He seemed larger than his average size and build with well-groomed, thick white hair.

George Hunt was quite comfortable in his old surroundings. He opened the conversation with, "Welcome, President Olson, can I call you Harold?"

"Please."

"I lobbied for your predecessor, which didn't turn out how I had hoped. I lobbied harder for you as the person I thought might salvage that debacle. In the interest of providing better context on the current state of affairs, have you met Chief Don Weston?"

"Only very briefly," Olson said, shaking hands with the chief.

"You need to get to know this man well. He's one of a few great assets that you've been gifted. I've asked him to take you on a quick walkabout of the campus. I think he can share some things that may provide greater meaning to our following visit."

"That sounds like ominously good guidance," said Harold.

"It won't take long," said George. "You already know the challenging financial situation of Churchville, like virtually every other small liberal arts college. Student life issues here also need attention that you wouldn't see on the surface or in the numbers. I'll wait for you and bask in the nostalgia of my old office."

In truth, George Hunt wanted to give Don Weston a chance to know the man, Harold Olson.

The tour began by stepping out into the impressive beauty of the Churchville campus. Idyllic is the best single word to describe Churchville University. Founded in the late 1800s, the campus is a beautiful mix of late 1800s and early 1900s architecture married to modern science and library/research facilities respectful of the original style. Giant live oaks and mature landscaping, along with the occasional hint of ivy, flow through the grounds. It's especially beautiful in the fall. The main, grassy quad of the campus is lined with pairs of red maples and hickory trees that turn to the school colors of crimson and gold in autumn, a nice detail attributable to a past president of the school: George Hunt.

"What's that?" Harold asked as they walked across the grounds towards the campus center building. He was pointing to a large metal sculpture. "It looks like a giraffe."

"Of the good, the bad, and the ugly, I'd say that's some of the good," he said as they walked up to the tree where a full-sized giraffe made of horseshoes was dining. "We're in the season for senior honors projects. This is part of an installation by one of the students. She is working with our resident artist sculptor on a menagerie. I imagine we'll see more similar wildlife dotting the campus as it progresses."

"What an incredible piece," remarked the new president. "I've always wished I had artistic talent. I like that a lot."

"Now, we'll see some of the bad," said Don. They entered the student union building, which housed the cafeteria. The cafeteria was open, but it was also full, with a long line of students waiting to get in. "This is normal at mealtimes, a consequence of your predecessor's moves to raise money by expanding the student body while cutting costs by shutting down several alternate food service venues."

Once outside, Don pointed out the multiple pleasing, if old, architectural edifices that made up student housing. "These are the original and current student dorms, there, there, there, and there. They were built with ample-sized rooms, each housing two student beds, desks, and closet space. Most of them have four to six bunks now."

"I guess this is our ugly after the good and bad?"

"Oh," said the chief. "You haven't heard the worst of it. The sanitary facilities were also designed for two-to-a-room occupancy. Additional fixtures have been added, but the lavatories are open rows of sinks, urinals, and uncloseted toilets. I've seen better accommodations in penal settings. That should be enough to give you the big picture." Don started back toward the president's office. Harold Olson, lost in thought, and possibly a beginning case of PTSD, had nothing to say.

Don said, "I've known George Hunt well and have a great deal of respect for his judgment, especially in the case of Churchville University. If he thinks you're the right guy to take the helm, I'm here for whatever you need. I understand we'll be weathering some rough seas."

Harold nodded. "I'll need to focus quickly on the financial strength and fundraising to keep the boat afloat. Fortunately, I have another resource to take on the needed administrative changes. I have the right person for that role in a woman my wife and I know well from our last school, Addison University."

How well? Don wondered. There's that cop sense sparking again.

"I'll leave you two to sort things out," said Don when they got back to George. "I need to follow up on a minor dorm altercation from last night. I suspect our combatants are best friends again this morning. I want to be sure of that," he said, smiling.

"I guess boys will be boys," said Harold Olson.

Don laughed this time. "True, but this one is a girl's dorm. See you fellows around the campus."

"Harold, welcome back," said a smiling George. "How was your trip with Chief Weston?"

"Informative, depressing, and mostly enlightening," was the quiet response. "I knew we had issues in the operating budget. I wasn't aware of the immediate financial need to repair the unacceptable student living conditions."

"Dr. Olson, the only options now are salvaging survival by increasing income and cutting costs. You're going to need to gain administrative support to make some hard changes."

Harold interjected, "I have to say that, while I've felt very welcomed here, I have sensed early roadblocks in discussions of change and choices, especially from the world of faculty leadership."

"I'm guessing you've met James Giles, the definition of resistance to change. I put him in the position of Academic Dean, believing once he was in that role, he was smart enough to begin to see the revisions we would need to make to stay competitive in the rapidly changing environment of higher education. I was wrong. My decision to place him in that office is badly in need of correction."

"My administrative plan is to introduce an organizational structure that entails a Provost position with division heads over grouped departments. In my experience at Addison, it was very effective in creating an environment of cross-divisional partnership."

"Harold, I think that's a great direction," George said. "Perhaps I could explore other opportunities for James that would support both the university and the religious affiliate. Dr. Giles is highly respected by our Mennonite community for his background and research in religious studies. I have some great connections there. Would you like me to pursue that?"

"Definitely," said Harold. "So, can you explain the past president? It seems he was an unusually bad fit here."

"That's my fault as well. He was everything I wasn't, and I thought the college needed just that. He was a corporate executive. Your predecessor dug into the financials immediately and spoke out loud about the bleak outlook. The board was deeply offended but also somewhat awakened. He was a smart guy, but his overbearing personality in the culturally foreign land of academic politics was never going to work. He was right about the financial situation but wrong in the approach to every intended solution."

"Well," said Harold, "I guess it's time for me to get to work."

And so, it began.

It wasn't long after President Olson's arrival that Dr. James Giles was ceremoniously, and unceremoniously, "promoted" to a grand leadership role in development at the university's religious affiliate. Not a dean. Not a department head. Not an influence in any Churchville University academic role.

The honeymoon period lasted less than a year. The personnel budget was next on the list.

PRESENT TIME

Isabel Helms

Isabel Helms was now the provost of Churchville University. She had served in that position for almost a year and was already universally regarded as an excellent administrator. She was initially rumored to have a special relationship with Harold Olson and his wife, Elly. Isabel's physical attractiveness—long dark hair and a tall, athletic build—only added to the speculation. Skepticism, gossip, and distrust are not abnormal welcoming committee traits at a small college.

Isabel's professional approach to the provost position and genuine openness and empathy with the faculty and the larger administration retired all of those concerns within six months of her arrival. She quickly and seamlessly established herself as well-qualified for the position and made work friends easily.

Today started out like any other day at the office. Morning light cascaded through the tall windows, highlighting and shadowing the comfortable furnishings throughout the architecturally historic administration building.

Isabel's admin, Alice Haywood, arrived to fresh brewed coffee. "Thanks, Isabel," she said. "I think I'm supposed to be making your coffee, but you always beat me to it," she laughed, joining Isabel at the small table in her office. Alice, a fifty-something widow, had weathered years of the Churchville experience, a great historian for Isabel through her transition.

"No problem," responded Isabel. "I'm happy to be of service." She also laughed.

"I've never had a boss say that to me before. You treat me more like a partner than an employee."

"Well, you are an excellent partner. I don't know what your previous working relationships have been like, but this is the only way I know to be."

"And I can't thank you enough for that," said Alice. "I wasn't sure I could go through another change here, and I was thinking about looking elsewhere. I'm glad I waited to meet you and get a new lease on work life. I used to drag my feet in the mornings, dreading the daily drudgery and confusion. Now I can't wait to get here for our morning coffee time. Anything new on the agenda?"

"Unfortunately, yes. We'll be doing faculty appraisals for much of the next few weeks. I'm working on the list for scheduling now. I'll need you to send the notices, schedule the conference room, and stock us with water, coffee, and basic light food offerings, like bagels and Danish."

"I guess we're having another 'purge' as the faculty refers to it. I've been through this before with my last boss, Dr. Giles. I know the school has some big challenges, but I find it sad when it affects people's lives."

"I do, too, it's not something anyone should take lightly. There are always situations that need to be addressed and even outcomes that can be positive for some of the involved individuals. There is also a litany of difficult conversations and collateral damages that deserve respect. It isn't numbers; it is people's lives."

"Dr. Giles seemed to enjoy it."

"I'm sorry to hear that. That must have been an uncomfortable work relationship for you."

"It was. He never involved me in any of the planning. I was here to make his tea the way he liked it and print out his emails so he could mark them up for me to send a response. He had his obvious favorites and his obvious targets, and he didn't desire anyone else's opinions on his choices."

"Do you keep in touch with him?"

"I probably should have told you this a long time ago. He called me a couple of months after you got here. I could tell he wasn't happy about the administrative changes at the school and was trying to check you out. He told me I should watch my back because you and the president were not to be trusted."

"Really?"

"Yes, I'm glad he waited a couple of months. I might have been scared if I hadn't already gotten to know you. Instead, I got a little pissed off. I told him you were the best boss I'd ever known, and I didn't need his opinion on that. He wasn't happy. He told me I should never talk that way to the dean of the college, and I'd find out soon he was right about you and the president. I guess he forgot we didn't have a dean anymore."

"I take it that conversation was out of character for your previous relationship."

"Absolutely. Maybe not for him but certainly for me. But it was also freeing and refreshing to put him off. To be honest, I never liked James Giles or anyone of his kind."

"His kind?"

"The kind that has to prove they're the smartest person in the room by being condescending and dismissive of others they think are beneath them, which is everyone."

The room went quiet.

"I'm sorry," said Alice. "That wasn't right for me to say, but it felt good."

Isabel broke the ice with her laughter. "It sounded genuine to me."

"It was, but now that I've said it, I never have to say it again."

"Alice, I'm flattered that you felt comfortable enough with me to share that. I want you to know that I appreciate your opinions on everything, especially when it comes to the people here. You've had years of experience with the faculty and the administration from a perspective that I'll never have. That is invaluable to me."

The conference room door opened, and Harold Olson and Don Weston wandered in. Harold's office shared the conference room space, and he usually stuck his head in about this time each morning to offer greetings. Don was also on his usual early morning track that regularly included Isabel and Alice.

"Good morning, ladies. How is everyone on this beautiful day?" Don asked.

"Good, Don, as always," said Isabel. "What brings the two of you together this morning?"

"Usual stuff," Don responded. Harold nodded.

"Well, Don, things are great now that you're here," said Alice. "Can I get you a coffee?" Alice was always extra pleasant in the company of Don Weston. For her, an age-appropriate widower was something to pay attention to.

"No time today, thank you. I have some pressing business with a faculty friend. The good doctor, Quinton Blackwell, has an issue with a student parking in his special reserved space."

"I wasn't aware we had special reserved parking spaces," commented Isabel.

"I wasn't either," added Harold. "Where is mine?"

"We don't, except apparently for Dr. Blackwell. He's summoned me to his office this morning to air his grievance. Should be a fun chat."

"Speaking of fun chats," said Isabel. "I need to summon you to a couple of the upcoming faculty evaluations. I don't expect any real issues, but I think your presence will be helpful in a few cases that may have a degree of elevated intensity."

"What a pleasant way to say 'frank and animated discussions with a potential for violent reactions,'" smiled Don.

"Dr. Olson will also be present for those potentially challenging interviews. I'll have Alice copy you on the scheduling for those."

"No problem," said Don. "I'm all yours for whatever you need. Keep me posted, Alice. I'm off to meet Dr. Blackman to deal with serious law enforcement priorities. You ladies have a wonderful day."

After Don left, Isabel remarked, "We're fortunate to have a professional like Don Weston here. He's certainly overqualified for our small campus, but I think that's exactly what we need for what we're about to face." That would turn out to be a profound statement.

REALITY IMPOSES
AT CHURCHVILLE

F aculty cuts were progressing with a great impact on the world of Isabel Helms. People were expensive. Forty percent of the faculty was tenured and seemingly protected, but their incomes had grown lofty in some cases, and retirement incentives were cooking away behind the scenes. Faculty still on the tenure track were easy to handle. James Giles's previous method of uncontested discharge for those deemed "non-academic" had returned, revised and tightened. This time his method would also touch the previously unaffected departments of English, Social Sciences, Art, Religion and Philosophy, and other "general ed" offerings.

Adjuncts, previously overlooked and not considered as anything but easily replaceable, were now the shining stars of the immediate future. The bright, sustainable future of the small, private Churchville University was starting to look like a majority faculty of adjuncts guided by a self-proclaimed, scholarly administration of surviving supporters. That was certainly not the intention of the president or provost, but it was a short- to mid-term reality of the current financial situation.

The last group of faculty at risk were the full-timers without tenure contracts. They were handled quickly before any of the other faculty assessments were scheduled. Harold Olson sat in on these and finally got to meet Glenn Weaver, the artist who was the architect of the horseshoe giraffe. The separation was bittersweet for Harold, but the financial formula had been agreed on, and this was one small part of it.

TESTING THE WATER

When Isabel had her weekend play dates, she never checked messages. Her immersion in the sublime—whoever and whatever she was living out—got her full attention. She was serious about her hobby. She got home late that Sunday, took a shower, and curled up with the iPad.

When she was caught up with her news links, social media, and personal emails, which wasn't much, she took her pre-bedtime ritual of checking Xnorml. It was her last transitional break from her awake time to bedtime, and she often found sleep dreams there. That night, she found a message in her inbox. That wasn't unusual, but the unfamiliar name was "Ironmansdungeon." Xnorml was a site for serious followers and participants of varying lifestyles, but her private profile did scare up the occasional lurking pervert. She wondered which this was.

It was one line: "Have you ever been strapped to a spinning wheel?"

She had not, but she'd seen them in pictures and even found one in an online lifestyle catalog, where $6,500 was the going price for pain or pleasure. She'd been to several first-class BDSM dungeons in the past couple of years, but none had the space, or likely the resources, to have a spinning wheel.

"No," she messaged back and went to bed.

BACK AT SCHOOL

Isabel entered Monday in a business suit and understated makeup. It would be a long morning of sometimes tense meetings with yet more faculty and staff, helping them understand their positions, or lack of positions, in the future of Churchville University. These were mostly held with just her, the appropriate division head, and her administrative assistant, Alice, as a witness.

In a few cases, such as a tenured faculty adjustment, she was joined by the university's legal counsel, Stewart Mason, or Harold Olson himself. The university was risk averse to any outside exposure of their future implementation, legal or otherwise. Don Weston was also asked to be on hand for a couple of the more potentially concerning interviews. Fortunately, Don's intervention had not been needed. Harold's presence, and personal persuasiveness, proved highly effective in the retirement cases. The authority to make any concessions or severance package adjustments was in the room.

The business day started early at 6:00 a.m. and ended at 4:00 p.m. Isabel had brought her gym bag with her and stopped by the women's locker room to change on the way to the tennis courts. The pre-tennis stretching and warmups started a little somber these days, but it only took a few good serves on the court to make the transition from work to relief.

In the truth of Don Weston's suspicions, unknown to the public world, Harold and Elly had always enjoyed the lifestyle of an open marriage. Elly was a natural flirt with both sexes, a petite vixen with long blond hair and an inviting nature. The open marriage relationship had expanded to a "throuple" in the Addison years with the company of Isabel. It was only natural that the three would become entwined.

Isabel Helms was single by choice. She had been an independent woman since she was eighteen years old. Isabel blossomed into adulthood as a very attractive woman, which she maintained carefully, always well-dressed, manicured, and perfectly assembled in total style. Men were drawn to her instantly, but she was not drawn to any attachment. By the age of twenty-one, Isabel decided that she would seek what she enjoyed where entanglements were universally shunned.

A good day on the court led to an even better day around the lemonade table at the president's house.

"What is with your game today, Isabel?" started Harold. "You thoroughly kicked my ass out there."

"I couldn't help myself," she said, wiping the sweat from her face. "Life is in a state of stress at the moment, and I needed an outlet. You just happened to be the unfortunate victim."

"All the time we've been playing, I've had more than a few hints you were better than you showed. It's been nice of you to keep your game down to my level of play so I could feel athletic. Today you confirmed my suspicions, shattering any last vestiges of a fragile male ego. If I didn't love and respect you and your athletic abilities so much, I'd brand you a bully."

"I do feel just a little bad about the beatdown," said Isabel.

"Not me," said Harold. "My only thoughts at this point are how we're going to find some unsuspecting doubles partners so I can win without trying too hard while I watch you pummel the competition."

Elly intervened. "You're both leaking too much testosterone on my patio. Time to lighten up, clean up, and relax."

Harold and Isabel hit the shower, and Elly joined them shortly in soapy play, transitioning to even more relief from the workday. The throuple lay naked on the bed together while Elly and Isabel told Harold all about their weekend activities. They had ventured out together this time, and the swinger parties were always a hoot. "I loved when you did that fat guy in front of his wife," said Elly with a smile. Isabel responded with a dirty laugh, "I loved it even more when you tied me to the bed and all three of you did me."

When the ladies did excursions on their own, Isabel tended to favor the online messaging rooms that explored the BDSM realm, and she continually upped her experience with contacts made there. While Harold and Elly didn't feel the same calling, a little soft bondage, feathers, maybe some ice, and the occasional blindfold could be fun. And they loved hearing the sordid and kinky details of the latest Isabel road trip.

Poor Harold lay there listening intently to the girls' successes. He had stayed alone all weekend, took real meetings, and wandered the large, lonely presidential mansion. He had read an old Carl Hiassen book to divert his thoughts from the school situation. There was just something about a mindless and forgettable Florida novel of wit and no wisdom to clear the head.

Isabel jumped up first. "Time to work on repairing the fragile male ego of the group," she announced, and the ladies proceeded to draw Harold out of his weekend drought.

HOME AGAIN

After a quick grab and go from a local restaurant, Isabel settled into her cottage retreat feeling somewhat better about the day. The personnel budget for the faculty was on track to resettle at a targeted, sustainable low. Further administrative adjustments were still pending but expected to go smoothly.

She wrote some poetry this evening, expanding on unfinished lines and even completing some sonnets. As the night approached, she followed her habit of news links, social media, personal emails, and checking Xnorml. Ironmansdungeon was in her inbox.

"There's nothing like it."

She could see Ironman himself was online. "Really?" she responded. She sat in the dark for a minute or more and then saw the . . . . . . symbols of a response being typed.

"Strapped naked to coarse lumber, blindfolded in a very hot dungeon; you could be in hell itself. Your guide cocks the wheel this way and that as your weight shifts and your equilibrium fades. Now, it works up slowly to full spins and total disorientation. He's hitting your hot flesh with alternating sensations of ice water, peacock feathers, wire ends, and any nature of stimulation until it stops suddenly. You don't know if you're up or down or if you're still moving."

"Hmmmm."

"Hmmmm, good?"

"Hmmmmm, very intriguing."

"I have a wheel."

Isabel hadn't dabbled this far in the BDSM lifestyle recently, keeping things light in her weekend forays. This sounded potentially delicious as a deeper dive into that pursuit, but she still didn't know if Ironman was for real, and she liked the idea of stringing this out for dream fodder. She could be patient in her fantasy construction, so Isabel signed off and went to bed.

As the school week progressed, so did Isabel's nighttime correspondence with the mysterious Ironman. On Tuesday evening, they engaged online again.

50shadesofunicorn: "Really, you have a wheel?"

Ironmansdungeon: "Why would I make that up?"

Ironmansdungeon: "I'd be pleased and proud to show it to you."

Ironmansdungeon: "Maybe you'd like to take it for a spin."

The one-liners progressed into details of the dungeon and a cautious vetting on both parts. Isabel was a relative novice in the real BDSM scene. She liked the thrill of the naughtiness, the feel of exposure and surrender, the "light touch" whipping, the bondage and submission. She had acquired some of her own tools in restraints and handcuffs and various instruments of external stimuli. She'd played with both Harold and Elly with some of these, but her ultimate interest in BDSM was the beyond-normal heightening of sensation that she liked to take to the sensual plane.

She pondered the Ironman's Dungeon scenario deeply, now convinced he was the real thing. The Wednesday Xnorml chat had surfaced that the Ironman's dungeon was a mere twenty-minute drive from the town of Churchville. You never knew where you might find the very small and secret world of the true adventurist lifestyle.

By Thursday evening, she had decided a spin might be fun after all. She'd get a new high. She still wasn't sure the sexual indulgence would be a part of a full BDSM master's desires, but she always had the safety and sensuality of her throuple triangle for relief and release. They'd love the story she could tell. Thursday evening's messaging set the logistics.

Ironmansdungeon: "Do you own a mask and hood?"

50shadesofunicorn: "Of course."

Isabel shared that this would be a big step beyond dipping a toe into the dark side. She also hinted that she was widely open to the clandestine and serious practice of the BDSM lifestyle. She was also open and hoping to find a sexual element to relieve her senses.

Ironmansdungeon: "I promise that when we have furthered your lifestyle experience, I will send you home, free of all cares and fully drained."

50shadesofunicorn: "Then, I think we're ready to do this."

Ironmansdungeon: "At 9 PM tomorrow, I will send a car for you. Be ready to step into your driveway when it arrives. You will be wearing the mask and hood. I must insist that you not see the driver, route, or location of your destination."

Ironmansdungeon: "Do you understand and agree?"

50shadesofunicorn: "I do."

Her heart thudded in her chest as she typed the two words. There would be no turning back now.

Ironmansdungeon: "Beyond the mask and hood, you should wear only a simple outer garment appropriate to the travel weather. There will be no need for undergarments. Bring your laptop and phone; I assume you have a laptop and a phone. We could have some very interesting files to share when we're together."

Ironmansdungeon: "Do you understand and agree?"

50shadesofunicorn: "I do."

Another commitment to the journey.

Ironmansdungeon: "Do you have a laptop and phone?"

50shadesofunicorn: "I do, an iPad actually."

Three times now.

Ironmansdungeon: "Be ready as instructed precisely at 9 PM tomorrow."

Ironmansdungeon signed off. Isabel went to bed to vivid but not unpleasant dreams.

FRIDAY

I sabel stopped by the office Friday morning to touch up some loose ends on the HR and budget front. It wasn't much, really, but she didn't enter her business sessions unprepared. When she was satisfied that she was ready for the next round of Monday HR activity, she left the office around noon and wandered over to the presidential mansion to check in with Harold and/or Elly. Both were home, having lunch.

"I'm cutting out early today. All is done for next week's contract talks, and I'm looking forward to a complete break from academia," announced Isabel. "My weekend starts tonight, and it will be a big one with a new and daring theme in the alternate lifestyle discipline. Be prepared to be astounded. What do you two have in the works?"

"Boring but fun," Elly said. "We're heading out as an old married couple on an unstructured schedule to do scenic drives and antiquing. I'm packing a bag so we can stay out somewhere if the mood strikes, but we're heading off to wander with no agenda." They were best friends. Fun conversation, road snacks, and just being in each other's company were a joy.

With Isabel's suggestion of naughty experimentation in her upcoming weekend, they briefly played a guessing game. Oddly, spinning wheels never came up in their otherwise imaginative stabs at the hint. Isabel kept mum, only saying that she'd see them for tennis and lemonade on Monday, and they should be prepared for a doozie.

They never saw her again.

FRIDAY NIGHT

When Isabel got home from school, she settled into a very long, hot bubble bath. She kept the drain lightly open and the faucet barely over a drip to maintain the glorious basking. She even took a small nap in bubbly luxury.

She walked to an early dinner at the Italian restaurant, a simple, small antipasto and a cannoli for dessert. Heading home at around 7:00, she took an inventory of the weather. It was a little overcast, but no precipitation was pending, and the night promised to be cooler than the day but not cold. She was used to packing for her weekend trips. A locked, antique wardrobe in her garage held the uniforms of her multiple other personas. It was a nice assortment of revealing dresses, cleavage-baring tops, high slits, and minis, along with a nurse outfit, red riding hood, and the usual lingerie for play-time. Also featured were some toys. She fingered one pair of hand-cuffs briefly, looked through some dresses, and departed with just the mask and hood.

At 8:00 p.m., she took a shower, thoroughly cleansing every ori-fice as she always did before an encounter. She always started ses-sions fresh, clean, shaved to perfection, and lightly perfumed in Tea Rose. She was a garden of delight. Time to pick the outfit for the eve-ning. She chose a pair of comfortable, slipper-like flats in case there was walking involved. On top of her glorious and firm body, she wore only a long London Fog raincoat. This is how it would be. At 8:55, she stood in her kitchen doorway, clutching her iPad and personal phone, watching for traffic.

At precisely 9:00 p.m., a small station wagon appeared, moving slowly. The lights were turned off as it entered her driveway behind

Isabel's car. The driver's door opened without any internal light. Isabel exited by the back kitchen door and didn't lock it. She rarely did unless she would be away for several days. She walked toward the driveway, fixed her mask over her eyes, and pulled the hood down into complete darkness. The mask alone would have done it, but the BDSM folks seemed to favor the hood in tandem. She was doing as she was directed without question. That was a part of the game. She stretched out her arms to feel her way forward. A small hand took hers, and a gentle male voice said, "I have you." Isabel felt an immediate comfort in the soft touch and reassurance. This was starting okay.

The driver and passenger made small talk about the weather and the local crops, always a safe discussion in a town with a past and current farming history. Isabel didn't know if he was part of the evening's entertainment or just a Lyft driver with a GPS. Isabel didn't ask, and the driver didn't offer. Still, the man never questioned her unusual choice of headwear, so he must know something.

The drive was short, much less than the projected twenty minutes. The man warned Isabel to be ready for the last mile. It was extremely bumpy and slow going, seemingly off-road to nowhere. The little station wagon slipped and gripped intermittently, at one point backsliding into a tree to the sound of breaking plastic and occasionally bottoming out completely with a crunching thud. This part might have been ten of the twenty minutes.

"I have you," the man with the soft voice and hands said again as he opened Isabel's door and took her by the hand. It was insanely quiet here. The driver led Isabel a short distance and opened what sounded like a large, sliding door. They had entered hell.

A powerful hand gripped Isabel's shoulder in welcome. "I am the Ironman," he said. "I've been looking forward to your visit." She heard the popping of what sounded like a wood fire, and the heat was intense. "We'll leave the door open for a while to drop the temperature while we prepare you for your night."

The chauffeur took Isabel's personal iPad and phone "for safekeeping," he said. She'd never mix business and pleasure, so her school laptop and phone remained at the house. Then, he was gone, and the large door closed to the sound of tires crunching on gravel and sticks as he drove away.

"Wasn't that my ride home?" asked Isabel.

"He'll return when it's time." But Ironman had told him that Isabel would not need a ride home.

Now, Ironman stood behind Isabel. He unbelted her London Fog from behind and pushed the big buttons through their holes. Gently pulling the coat from her shoulders, he now exposed Isabel completely to whatever and whoever was in the room. She could feel that he was wearing a hard, leather suit—maybe coveralls. He told Isabel she wouldn't be needing her shoes and collected them with the coat.

"Would you like to see the wheel?" he asked.

"I guess that's why I'm here," she responded. Rough fingers pulled the hood to the top of her head and dropped the mask just enough to see ahead where the wheel stood. It was a truly impressive creation to behold, much like an oversized wagon wheel supported upright, leaning away from her at a forty-five-degree angle. The detail was inviting.

There were blocks for footholds at the bottom edge with leather, buckled straps to secure the rider. More leather straps were at the sides, approximating a cross. Isabel had expected her arms to be high over her head, but this looked much more comfortable for a ride. In the center was a soft pad that would support her backside, another surprising touch of comfort. It looked like the actual attachment of one's body would be more like a piece of gymnastics equipment than a torture device. She didn't expect she'd regret this at all.

The mask and hood were tucked securely back in place. The only other sight of her brief look revealed what she thought was some sort of a warehouse filled with unusual equipment and neatly stacked piles of junk. She'd also noted that the base of the wheel was set in a large, plastic kiddie swimming pool, filled with something. She'd soon know more as the man took her hand and led her closer.

"Watch your step," he said as he brought her over the lip of the swimming pool to touch down in a loose, but not uncomfortable, surface of large sand or small gravel, already an interesting skin sensation for the blind. He helped her to climb on the wheel, carefully guiding her backside to the padded surface and her hands and feet to their respective places.

Feet first, he buckled her in. She noticed another surprising detail in a tapered notch just above the foot blocks. When the soft leather was pulled, tied, and secured, her left heel was comfortably in the notch, allowing her calf to fit against the device as tightly as her ankle. She could feel her vagina opening as he spread her right leg to the other foot block and repeated the ritual.

The arms were next, each secured by the same soft leather in two places, one strap at the wrist, the other above the elbow. With the pad behind her, it was not at all uncomfortable. Lastly, a final restraint was looped around her neck. This one was the same leather but with a lining that was very soft against her skin. She was briefly about to break character, but then it was explained that this one stayed loose, controlling the weight of her head as the ride commenced but retaining inches of slack. She realized this strap was in her control and thought she might even want to press against it for an autoerotic addition to her senses.

"You are ready to begin," the man said. "We'll now raise you to get started." There was a mechanical ratcheting as the entire wheel rose, bringing her to an upright position, weight on her feet and her straps.

With Isabel still securely blinded, the promised rocking began. And the heat grew more intense. Her hips and her free breasts swayed with the wheel's movement as it went ever higher. The room was so hot. She remained silent, fully submissive.

More rotation continued to greater plateaus on the geometric scale, building a fascinating feeling of sense deprivation and sense awakening at the same time. She allowed herself to lean into the soft neck collar and heighten the stimulation with light and controlled self-choking. She was in total submission, blinded and strapped, but she took control of the neck collar. The rocking by hand had almost completed a circle by now, and a powered device was clicked into place against the frame of the giant disc. Now, she spun completely, very slowly. This truly was a sensation like no other. Rolling into darkness in the heat of Hades, her sweat spun off in all directions as she also felt the slightly cooling, condensing effect of the motion.

The speed and effect increased slowly at first. This was the greatest carnival ride ever. It accelerated to a steady whoosh, whoosh, whoosh, of fiery wind. Her wet hair flew recklessly. Her hips and breasts were uncontrolled as she leaned harder into the neck collar. When she was completely devoid of any sense of direction, she felt small darts piercing her flesh. The darts were random streams of ice water under pressure. They struck her arms, her legs, her stomach, and her neck. They also found her nipples and exposed vaginal cavity with uncanny accuracy. This was joined by another delicious torture; feathers and loose cords haphazardly whipped her skin while she whirled at high speed. The great torture/pleasure machine experience was a complete surrender to touch and feel and a loss of all being that never stopped in her mind, even as she became unconscious.

When she awoke, the machine was still, but she was far from still inside. In her head and gut, the spinning continued, quietly now. She was sweating heavily in the heat of the fire and didn't care. She was truly unaware of her position, head up, head down—there was no point of reference for anything stable. She was missing the water jets and soft whips, but she knew she couldn't take them anymore. Light red stripes from their invasion crisscrossed her body. She couldn't see them, but she could trace their trails in her mind, the stings supercharged with alert nerve ends everywhere. Glorious sensations. He hadn't lied.

In the dark quiet, a soft, vibrating dildo entered her sweaty vagina, followed in course by larger and firmer intruders. This was the next step she truly craved. In the environment of her scrambled thoughts, the sexual pleasure was intense, very welcome, and enjoyed deeply. She'd been dilated before in her BDSM play and didn't mind this transition at all. Next came an unfamiliar, coarser object and the fingers that held it. She was being virtually fisted in a screwing, stretching invasion that opened her up until she groaned loudly, with both pain and pleasure.

And then, the hand pushed the button on the object, releasing the OTF switchblade through the top of her vaginal opening, her uterus, and into her intestines. From this moment on, Isabel could only hope for the death that would come soon. She screamed, begged, prayed, and cursed, all in the deep woods, where no one could hear.

He'd promised to send her home again, free of all cares and fully drained. He hadn't lied.

FRIDAY, SATURDAY, AND ON

As Isabel's life and soul dripped, dripped, dripped into the six inches of kitty litter in the swimming pool on Friday evening, Ironman opened the big bay door of the newly-christened torture chamber to the refreshing night air and gathered his tools to begin the final finishes and cleanup. She'd bled an impressive amount already but was still annoyingly alive, slipping in and out of consciousness with occasional, convulsive thrashing and whining noises.

He was glad he had left her mask and hood in place. He doubted she could identify him, but he didn't care to share his face, and the hood helped muffle the noises from her head. His artistic sense kicked in to speed things up with some further perforations. The razor-sharp knife that had made the vaginal journey now moved to her breasts. Large, deep smiles were carved below the beautiful melons. A surprising amount of blood still pumped from her body. Her wrists were opened next, producing a fountain of arterial spurting, marking each heartbeat, the big pool and the kitty litter consuming all. The neck was the last cut, an OJ/Nicole beauty that would be the precursor to removing the head. In very short order, the spurting and dripping subsided from all the wounds. When her bowels were released, he knew she was gone.

Time to start cleanup and disposal. He cut the leather retaining straps and the neck collar to let the carcass drop into the kitty litter. He pulled the hood and mask to see an expressionless face with dead shark eyes looking at nothing. The straps went into the big wood stove. The shoes and raincoat had already made that trip when Isabel was spinning into unconscious bliss.

He lovingly disassembled the giant wheel, bit by bit. It was a proud piece of work, but it was built for only one showing and no longer needed. The wood was fed to the fire gods, and the metal pieces went back to the scrap pile. The pool and its contents remained where the wheel once stood. The iPad and phone were the next priority.

Isabel would not be missed for long. Her whereabouts would certainly be in question by Monday, possibly as soon as tomorrow. Certainly, a search of her home would be a first step, and it wouldn't do for someone to find her outside correspondence as the Ironman had, especially since it now contained communication with him. Even with a VPN, he didn't doubt that a true expert could follow that path. The iPad, its cord, and the phone were cut into small pieces with a plasma cutter. He kept the knife. He'd need it again.

There were always some coals in the kilns with a constant and adjustable gas feed. He prepped the ceramic kiln for work. A potter's kiln for ceramics could reach 2500 degrees, almost a thousand more degrees than the fire of a crematorium. After a little effort in the pool, the head went in first. So did the remains of the iPad. Through the next two days, Saturday and Sunday, various sizes of other butchering followed, sending the sweet smell of meat cooking into the sky to dissipate through the forest. Flesh disappeared quickly, and the bones, made into small pieces by the plasma cutter, were now brittle from the heat of the furnace. Putting the little remaining pieces between two thick, steel plates under a metal press crushed them to dust easily.

By Monday, there were only ashes spread in a nearby garden with the contents of the pool. The tiny pellets of dry clay were quite good for the soil and plants. The clumps in the kitty litter were soon gone, quickly found by various wildlife. The pool was rinsed with bleach, as were the metal plates from the press, and everything was stored away for no good reason. The universe had forever lost any thread of living DNA that marked the existence of Isabel Helms.

His work here was done for now.

DON WESTON

College life had slowed things down on the law enforcement front for Don. It was a welcome change since his retirement from a long career in urban policing. There were the usual parking violations, drunk and disorderly, and some drug incidents. One also encountered the occasional Title IX investigations. Those were never fun and often not clearly resolved, with much hearsay and the usual involvement of alcohol. What he really liked, though, was that Churchville was a small campus, but its students were not commuters, so it was more like a small town.

Crowd control at a D3 football game was less taxing than Philadelphia fireworks on Independence Day. During last semester's football season, Don was overseeing the entry gate when Harold and Elly Olson arrived. "Ready for a break?" asked Harold.

"If it's a break to grab some food, I'm always ready. I'm so hungry, I could eat a double dog if they had such a thing."

"We're just making the stadium rounds," said Elly, "until we get settled in at the president's box. You should join us when the game gets started."

"When things quiet down here, I have a few undergrads to look in on, but I'll be able to stop in sometime in the first quarter."

"I hate to disappoint you on the meal," said Harold. "We're only serving prime rib at that venue."

Don laughed, "I guess I'll have to make do, see you in a bit."

When the bulk of the crowd had entered, Don made his way to the hotdog stand at the stadium.

"Good to know where you boys are this evening," he said as he approached the stand.

The concession was run by the baseball team as a fundraiser. Don knew the players well, having detained a number of them recently for an expensive incident of vandalism on the ball field.

"No donuts tonight, Chief," said Steve Dempsey. A bystander might have taken that as a jab at the stereotypical police diet, but Don and Steve knew it was a reference to the drunken evening when several of the team members ran their cars in circles on the baseball diamond.

"How is your dad doing?" asked Don. Steve's father had been more than a little frustrated with his son when Chief Weston presented him with the $8,000 bill for the field repairs.

"Let's just say it may be some time before I'm considered the number one son again. But he and the other guy's parents still think you're the number one cop for managing to keep us all out of jail and in school after what we did." The other players working the stand joined in a round of applause.

"I hoped it was more of a teachable moment than a time to ruin your lives. Institutional vandalism over $5,000 constitutes a felony in this state. That, with a record of school expulsion, would follow you forever."

"Lesson learned," chimed in another one of the offenders. "We can't thank you enough for how you handled things. We certainly deserved whatever punishment came our way. The opportunity to make a public apology and restitution for our stupidity will never be forgotten."

"Hard to believe, but I was young and stupid once," said Don. "I think a second chance for young and stupid is usually in order when possible. But never a third one."

"I can assure you none of us will ever be before you or the school administration again, unless we're accepting awards for baseball or community service."

Steve handed Don a wrapped hotdog. "This one's on the team," he said. "We won't let you down."

As Don unwrapped the dog at the condiment stand, he was astonished to see it was, in fact, a double dog. He glanced back to the counter where the boys were laughing. How did they know?

HELEN'S ADVICE

Don Weston had another very personal reason for slowing life down. He often thought back to meeting his wife when they were both graduate students at Temple. Don was already established with the Philadelphia Police Department, and Helen was a nurse at Temple University Hospital.

Their careers complemented each other well. They knew each other's stressors. They applauded the successes and consoled the tragedies that were inherent in their chosen professions. The one thing that proved to be difficult was working in a family. They both wanted children, but the pressures and schedules necessitated cautious thought on how and when to introduce that stage of life. Still, they were young and had lots of time to figure that out.

Until they didn't.

They had been married for fifteen years when, just before Christmas, Helen developed a debilitating shoulder pain that wouldn't go away. The source was a tumor on her left lung. She had small-cell lung cancer that had already metastasized to her bones and her brain. Helen was gone in mere months, and Don was alone. Don coped with his loss by distancing himself from life and plans with Helen. He took up his Civil War hobby to travel and focus on anything else, and he put every remaining ounce of energy into his work to stay occupied.

Eventually taking his retirement and moving to Churchville meant Don was entering into a new world. Job stress would diminish, and his hobby would flourish, both positive outcomes. The most positive outcome was that he was now surrounded every day by a campus full of vibrant young people, the same ages that he and

Helen's kids could have been. That was the biggest reward of retirement and also the biggest hole in his heart that Helen couldn't be there with him.

Another big hole in Don's heart was the nagging feeling that Churchville University, as beautiful as it was on the outside, had begun to erode on the inside.

Don hoped for the best, but he was also preparing for another retirement and an expansion of his consulting work. He loved the physical place he was in. He loved the students. He wasn't a fan of the politics. Don was still coping by staying busy. He was currently working on plans for his biggest weekend of the semester.

"Helen," Don said out loud as he sat in his big chair at home. "What are your thoughts on the resignation letter?"

Don talked with his wife Helen often. He knew she was dead and gone for years. Don didn't believe that Helen heard and responded to him when they talked. He wasn't a religious and spiritual guy in that sense. But he did believe that somehow a special part of her lived on in him. He chose to think that her influence guided his conscience and reflection, a sounding board for the small struggles and big decisions. He listened carefully, even knowing that he was answering for himself.

Don, said the voice of Helen. *Why did you write that letter? You've told me these are the best times of your life. You love being surrounded by the students that could have been our children if we had been blessed with that gift.*

"Yes, but ..."

But what? Why would you give that up?

"I also miss the days when my work was filled with action, when I was a real cop chasing the bad guys."

We know that's never coming back. We're too old for that. What's the real reason for quitting now?

"It's all changing. The administrative drama since George retired is sad. Did I ever tell you what George said when we first met?"

I don't think so, tell me now.

"'I heard about you,' said George, 'from some friends, if one can call a Philadelphia lawyer a friend. For now, I need a campus police chief, but soon I think a partner with your skillset could be ideal to help me navigate some other campus issues, specifically my transition to retirement.' So I knew going in what was coming. George let me know the troubles the school would be facing, but somehow, when he was still there, it seemed safe and comfortable. Once he left the day-to-day of Churchville, I've seen many great teachers and friends, who loved these students as I do, simply cast aside, often just because they rightfully questioned some of the direction of the school."

What would you do with your life if you weren't here at Churchville?

"Maybe I could take on a chief job at a large school like Penn State. Maybe adding some actual police work action back into my life would perk things up."

Well, what is it then, Don? Do you need action, or do you want to run away from administrative drama? I think you know that the latter would accelerate rather than evaporate at a larger school. Have you honestly thought that through?

"Convicted," said Don.

Do you think the new leadership at the school is bad?

"Actually, no. I think they're facing the reality of survival in a painful but practical way. Things will certainly feel worse before they get better, but I think Churchville can survive and grow. There could be a brighter future here."

Wouldn't you like to be a part of that? Wouldn't that be better than giving up something you love to chase something unknown and uncertain?

"Helen, I have some nagging thoughts about these new folks."

You've told me you find them very professional and competent. You've also told me before that you sense some relationship beyond the professional. Does that matter to the school or you personally?

"Honestly, no. Just nagging thoughts."

Don, I don't think you want to quit. Making a new change to run away from these changes doesn't seem to make the best sense to me. Don't you have your annual big trip for your Civil War thing coming up?

"I do."

Would you promise me you'll enjoy that time and give up on this resignation thing for now? Take some "Don" time with your friends and see how you feel after a break. We can talk about it then.

"You always have the best advice. I promise. No doubt we'll be talking again soon. Love you, Helen."

For the past ten years, a group of amateur Civil War buffs had been meeting at a farm outside Gettysburg. They took the same VRBO rental every year, most arriving on a Friday. Some slept in tents as reenactors, others just hung out. The highlight was the group walk of Pickett's Charge on Saturday morning. This year was especially fortuitous for Don as it coincided with the first weekend of Spring Break. He and some of the group from Pennsylvania were planning to travel on to Antietam and down into the Shenandoah Valley the following week. This should be the perfect break for Don to unwind, relax, and step away from his current thoughts, but things were about to get complicated.

THE AFTERMATH
OF ISABEL

Today did not start out like any other day at the office.
Early Monday morning came, and Isabel Helms' office was curiously dark and empty. She was always in before the staff, generating notes and directions for guidance and tasks. The coffee hadn't been started when her administrative assistant, Alice Walker, arrived. Alice hadn't remembered anything on Isabel's schedule that would explain her absence but set about making coffee and getting ready for the day's meetings, expecting Isabel anytime now.

When nothing was heard by 9:00 a.m., Alice began canceling the day's schedule and was getting concerned. Harold Olson stopped by to say good morning.

"Dr. Olson," asked Alice. "I haven't seen Dr. Helms this morning. Do you know if there was anything else she might have had to do this morning?"

"You know her work schedule better than any of us. I know I didn't have any meetings with her this morning until we start our faculty interviews."

"I've already canceled the morning meetings. I tried her cell and home phone and sent an email and text an hour ago with no response."

"I hope things are okay. It's not like her to not be here ahead of us." He was initially as puzzled as Alice, but he also remembered that his friend had hinted at big things for the weekend. He smiled inside, thinking that she had extended unannounced, expecting to hear from her soon and greatly looking forward to the after-tennis story session.

But 3:00 p.m. came and went with no sign of his tennis partner. Harold called Alice. "Have you heard from Isabel?"

"Not a word. I'm concerned."

"Me too."

"What should I do?"

"Don't worry, I'm sure she's okay. Why don't you cancel Isabel's Tuesday schedule for now, and we'll sort it out when she shows up? Take the rest of the day off, and I'll call you at home when she checks in."

"Thank you," Alice responded, wiping away a tear.

Sitting at the outdoor table with the pitcher of lemonade, Harold and Elly weighed the disappearance carefully. They were deeply confused and concerned for Isabel and themselves. They were unexpectedly missing the third leg of their stool and scarily off-kilter.

"Harold, I'm afraid," said Elly.

Don Weston was working on plans for his Gettysburg trip when the phone rang. "Dr. Olson," he answered. "What's up?"

"Isabel is missing. She had meetings scheduled all day, and we had our regular tennis date at 3:00. Nobody has seen or heard from her."

"Hmmm, Alice called about noon to tell me Dr. Helms hadn't shown up today. I thanked her for the call about the unusual absence but suggested she wait things out for a little while. I was fully expecting a story of a flat tire or misfunctioning alarm clock. I hadn't heard back from Alice and assumed all was well."

"I thought the same until she didn't show up for our tennis time and didn't call. What should we do? Elly has a key to her house. Should we go look for her?"

"You and I may do just that, but let me get some official balls rolling first. You and Elly sit tight and wait to hear from me. I'm on it."

Hearing a simple "I'm on it" from Don was enough for Harold and Elly to seek some element of calm.

THE HUNT FOR ISABEL BEGINS

Monday and Tuesday

Don Weston hung up from the president's call and made several more of his own. The TV folklore that you can't file a missing-person report for 24 hours is simply a myth in most jurisdictions, but this was not yet an official report anyway. Don was making courtesy calls to the Churchville town police and Sheriff Bill Hester at his York County Department. He was a highly respected colleague of both.

He informed his local law-enforcement contacts that he'd appreciate it if they could put this on their respective and collective radars. The absence of Isabel Helms was technically only eight hours old. It was also completely and entirely out of character, and, as such, he let them know he would take an initial canvas of college security monitors and told them he'd appreciate a call if they saw or heard anything. He went a step further with an additional heads up to another old contact, Lieutenant Colonel Lester Timmons, director of the Pennsylvania State Police Bureau of Criminal Investigation based in Harrisburg.

Don had made many connections throughout his career. He spent years as the Philadelphia task force coordinator. That linked him closely with the other police units in the city from the Transit Department to various military branches and the FBI. Local counties, primarily Montgomery, Bucks, and Chester, but ranging to Lancaster and York, were daily contacts, as was the Pennsylvania State Police.

Don now called the Olsons back. Elly answered.

"Elly," he said. "Do I understand that you may have a key to Dr. Helm's house?"

"I do."

"Can I come by to pick you and Dr. Olson up in a couple of minutes? I think it would be prudent to do a quick check on the provost's residence. I can explain details on the way."

"We'll meet you in the driveway with the key."

Don started with instructions as the Olsons got into his police cruiser.

"If Dr. Helms does not show up by tomorrow morning, I've already made arrangements for law enforcement resources to join in a more thorough search of this house tomorrow. Let's hope that the provost simply got her dates crossed up and all of our potential concerns go away overnight. Right now, we are doing a welfare check. I am acting as a friend of a friend checking on a friend. I need the two of you to not come inside when we get to the house and trust me. Can you promise me you'll do that?"

"Whatever you say," said Elly. "We trust you."

That lasted until they pulled up in front of the house and saw Isabel's car in the driveway.

"Yay!" shouted Elly as she jumped out of the car. "She's home!"

Don's suddenly stern cop voice stopped Elly in her tracks. "Elly, Harold, I can't express strongly enough why we need to move a step at a time here. Do not go any further or touch anything on this property unless I tell you it's okay."

"But she's home now," pleaded Elly.

"I hope you're right. Give me the key and we'll find out, but stay here by my car right now."

Don knocked loudly on the front door and waited. No response. The door was locked, and he entered with the key. "You two stay where you are. I'll be right out."

"If she's not here, should we tell him about her weekend plans?" Harold asked Elly when Don had gone inside.

"Are you prepared to tell him everything else? I'm scared, Harold," said Elly, brushing away tears. "I know you are, too, but we have to trust that Isabel is okay."

"I know. It's likely unrelated, so I guess it makes sense to wait and see." He hugged her as he tried to think of a way to sort things out.

It was a small house with an open floor plan, so Don could quickly see that no one was home and nothing seemed out of place. He also saw some items that led him to believe that all was not well. He wouldn't share that with the Olsons. There would be a more thorough look with proper attention to evidence procedures tomorrow if Isabel was still missing. Don was pretty sure she wasn't coming home. He locked the door with the key.

Back at the cruiser, he informed the Olsons they were done for the evening.

"Dr. Helms is not at home. There is no sign of forced entry. There's no sign of any altercation. There is no sign of a crime scene at this home. Having said that, if she doesn't show up at the office tomorrow, I'll be back here with evidence technicians to thoroughly process the residence. I couldn't take the chance that one of you might have inadvertently compromised the scene. I hope you understand."

"We get it," said Harold. "We'll hope for the best, but if something has happened to Isabel, we wouldn't want to get in the way of whatever you need to do to find out."

Don dropped them off and did a little more office time that evening. Churchville campus security under Don's guidance had become a sophisticated net of cameras that covered virtually all possible common area and facility hallway views. From open spaces and athletic fields to residence halls and classroom buildings, nothing went unrecorded. All monitored activity was saved in thirty-day loops of time. It wouldn't take long to review the footage of the past few days. Don Weston personally began that process from his office.

THE HUNT FOR ISABEL

Tuesday

Tuesday morning, Alice arrived to find Isabel's office dark yet again. She was in tears when Harold stopped by on his good morning rounds.

"No sign of Isabel?" Harold asked, already knowing the answer.

"Dr. Olson, I'm scared that she may be in real trouble. She would have called if she could."

"Chief Weston and I visited her home yesterday evening. She wasn't there, and there were no signs of trouble at her house. He's alerted local and state law enforcement to be on the lookout, and he's going back today to look for more."

Composing herself, "I feel better knowing that Don is involved. If there's a simple answer, he'll find it out."

"I'm going to suggest you cancel Isabel's appointments for the week. It will be easy enough to reschedule when she is back."

"I'll do that now."

"When you wrap that up, why don't you take the day off and go home? I'll let you know what's happening as things progress."

"Thank you, Dr. Olson, but I think I'll feel better if I stay on campus. I think I'd just worry and cry if I were on my own. There is plenty I can do here, and I'd rather dive into work to stay occupied. How is your wife doing with this? I know she and Dr. Helms are very close."

"Thanks for asking. Elly is following your path, trying to stay occupied until we know more. She and Isabel are closer than sisters, it's a very special relationship." After a long pause and with a slight crack in his voice, Harold muttered, "I should be going now." He turned away so Alice wouldn't see the tears in his eyes.

All parties still held hope that Isabel would walk in the door at any moment.

Don finished his search of the relevant security footage that morning. The results were unremarkable, save some nighttime footage showing two inebriated lacrosse players urinating on a dorm building and a couple canoodling on the university logo in the middle of the football field. Absolutely nothing showed up from building hallways or common areas that showed Isabel on campus since Friday afternoon.

Shortly after noon, he was back at Isabel's house. Don waited briefly to be joined by an officer from the town police force and two law-enforcement personnel from the County Sheriff's Office. Sherriff Hester had sent a detective, Rick Walker, and an evidence technician. Don knew Rick well and was glad to welcome him as a partner.

Detective Rick Walker of the York County Sheriff's Department had a part-time diversion as an adjunct professor at York County Community College. Don considered him a friend, and Rick had recently asked Don if he would consider team-teaching a future class on cold cases.

Don gathered the group and gave them their instructions. "There is no hard evidence to mark this as a crime scene, but it will be treated as such while I'm in charge of this investigation. There is no search warrant, and we are still operating in the role of a welfare check for now. I expect that will change after this visit, but we need to respect the legal guidelines of our situation. We will take finger-prints, gather potential DNA samplings, and recover some evidence seen on my visit last evening. I'll take responsibility for any pending legal questions on those three issues. As a university employee, I can argue some leeway that the rest of you don't have without a warrant. Everyone will wear plastic field gloves throughout our time here, and those will be changed if anything has been handled. We'll also take pictures of everything.

"I know you're all professionals here. You may think I'm operating with an overabundance of prudence, but I've seen too many cases of clues lost forever to a lack of caution. Your role will be to assist me with a thorough visual inspection of the house and grounds. If you identify any potential evidence that should be secured, I will do the physical handling of it. Let's start outside."

The entire lot was walked off, looking for anything: tire tracks, loose refuse, footprints, evidence of a peeping tom or forced entry, or tools that would be valuable if found. Nothing. The evidence technician proceeded to dust all outside entry points of the house and garage for any fingerprints and produced results at all points. These would be preserved and reviewed.

"Pay special attention to dusting the back kitchen door," said Don. "I saw on my visit here last night that it was unlocked and left it untouched. It would be the presumed point of entry."

When the outside review of the grounds was completed, the group followed Don and cautiously entered through the front door, using the key supplied by Elly Olson. A cursory look showed nothing out of place or changed since Don's visit the day before.

The great room areas looked normal for the home of a single woman. Office area, various reading materials, and contemporary, comfortable furniture. The evidence technician set up bright lighting on tripods for a deep inspection of the carpeting, but nothing unusual was found. Isabel kept her home very clean. They moved to the bathroom and bedroom next. Nothing unusual or alarming. The closet was well organized. Isabel's clothes, mostly business attire, were pressed and hung neatly. Shelves had been added for shoes and sportswear, and all appeared in order. The local town cop let out a small giggle when he found Isabel's vibrator in the drawer of her nightstand.

"Might I remind you," Don Weston said sternly. "That we're viewing a potential crime scene for a missing and possibly endangered person? Your only thoughts should be for potential evidence in the article itself."

"Sorry, Chief Weston, I was just surprised. I didn't mean anything by it."

"No harm, no foul," said Don as he placed the article in the bag supplied by the evidence technician to save it for potential fingerprint and DNA research.

Rick Walker called to Don from the bathroom search. "We have a hairbrush with trace follicles and some visible hair at the tub drain." Don changed his gloves and collected the brush and the drain samples.

The only room left in the house was the kitchen.

"I've saved the kitchen for last," Don announced. "Based on the car in the driveway and the personal effects in this room, my operating assumption is that Isabel Helms willingly left the residence but did not leave here on her own and is not now likely to return on her own. Rick, I'm especially interested in your thoughts as we go through this final room."

Rick opened cabinets and made notes with a fifteen-minute inspection of the room. "I think I've already made the same assumption," he said. "My general observation is no dishes in the sink and nothing appears to be disturbed or out of order. Cabinet and refrigerator contents are sparse and normal for a single person living alone. The unlocked kitchen door would be consistent with no personal safety concern and possibly an intention to return soon. Based on the potential victim's car in the driveway, one might expect she left the house with another person, seemingly trusted. No evidence of a crime scene."

"Except?" prompted Don.

"What woman leaves their house without their keys, purse, and cell phone, all here on the kitchen table?"

"Bingo," said Don. "I also know that cell phone is not her personal phone. It's the one issued by the school. And she never goes anywhere without that leather organizer, also left behind. It wouldn't appear that our friend Isabel planned to be gone for even hours, let alone days." The contents of the table were bagged for further inspection, and the house search was pronounced dome for now.

The garage was normal. It was not used for vehicle storage, but other items were present. There were some skis, a small kayak, paddles, and various accompanying pieces and accessories common to the outdoor activities of an athletic woman. There was an old wardrobe cabinet to one side. It was secured with a hasp and padlock. None of the keys on the key ring from the kitchen fit the lock, and it was left undisturbed for now.

Isabel's Prius was parked in the driveway. It was locked, but they had the fob on her key ring. Entry and common touch-point surfaces were dusted, and samples were pulled with clear tape. They were hoping to find some history here, but the navigation system had no saved previous locations, only home.

Detective Rick Walker and Don Weston agreed that the best resource for processing the evidence and isolating DNA would be the Pennsylvania State Police Bureau of Criminal Investigation. Don made a call to Lester Timmons from the scene, and arrangements were put in place for an expedited review of the materials. The house, garage, and vehicle were sealed pending further inspection.

Don called Harold Olson next. Harold answered with, "Don, anything new?"

"Nothing we didn't already know yesterday, but we did gather some articles for the state police lab to review. Still no evidence of foul play, but I'd like to use your conference room beginning tomorrow to start interviews. I'll be joined by a York County detective to document Isabel's work schedule and habits as a starting point."

"Anything you need, Don. Consider Alice your admin for contacts and scheduling at the school. I'll let her know as soon as we hang up."

INTERVIEWS

Wednesday

This was now an official missing-person case. The campus police department had full police powers and jurisdiction but limited resources for a full investigation. The county and state were on call and committed to whatever Don Weston needed. All parties agreed there was no evidence of foul play at this point. The jurisdiction of investigation remained at the campus level, unless or until more evidence surfaced or more help was needed.

Don had the executive conference room for interviews. It was located between the provost and president's inner offices with access from both and a third door in the hallway. It was equipped for audio and video recording. Interviews would be conducted by the already involved and experienced York County detective, Rick Walker, and Chief Don Weston.

Rick Walker was very familiar with Churchville University, but this was the first time he had visited the offices of the senior administration. "Wow," he gasped on entering. He was surrounded by walls of dark wood wainscotting. Details of birds-eye maple inlay contrasted with the mahogany to mirror and complement the giant gleaming maple table. Large rocking and rolling armchairs were overstuffed and clad in yards and yards of green leather. "Nice interrogation room," he said.

"I don't know," said Don. "I thought the ones in Philly with the metal table and chairs and the bolts in the floor and walls for securing handcuffs had much more charm."

"Point taken. There is a potential to lose focus in surroundings like this."

"I've lost consciousness in these surroundings more than once sitting in one of those big chairs while some academic blathered on about epistemology and pedagogy."

"I guess we'll just have to make do as best as we can."

"The standard bagels and Danish arrive at 9:30. Drinks are in the fridge in the corner next to the wet bar."

Just then Harold Olson entered from his office to make sure things were in place.

"Welcome, Dr. Olson," greeted the chief. "I'd like you to meet Detective Rick Walker from the York County Sheriff's Department. Rick will be a key partner in our ongoing investigation."

"Very nice to meet you, Rick. We appreciate all the support we can get in finding Isabel. She is unquestionably the backbone of Churchville academics and a good friend to myself and my wife." Harold was a little nervous. He couldn't stop thinking about Isabel's weekend encounter and whether or not it was important to her disappearance. He just wasn't ready to face the questions that might arise. "Is there anything I can do to be of assistance?"

"Chief Weston and I will be following a well-established protocol of research. We may need your help gathering resources or removing roadblocks along the way. I promise we won't be slow or shy in asking."

"I'll do whatever I can. I guess the first thing I can do is get out of the way so you guys can get started."

"Thanks," said Don. "We'll keep you filled in on any new details."

When Harold left, Rick asked, "Is he a suspect? He seems a little anxious."

"Isn't everyone and everything at this point? But my instinct says the Olsons' concern is genuine. I'd consider them as only very peripheral suspects until we know more. Isabel has been with Churchville for almost a year, but Harold and his wife, Elly, have a much longer relationship with her. They had been social friends at Addison University in Ohio, where she and Dr. Olson had been peers. I hadn't planned to include them in our first round of interviews. I've spent much time with them, particularly in the past two days, and already gathered their information on Isabel's work habits, tennis schedule, etc."

"Anything I need to know from that?"

"For background, which I've already verified, I learned from Elly Olson that Isabel Helms has no family. She was an adopted, only child, and her parents died in a plane crash near the end of her senior year in high school. Their neighbors, a retired couple, took her in for just over a month, and then she was off to college on a full academic scholarship. The neighbors had also passed on in the ensuing years. The Olsons have always known her to be a creature of habit, early to bed and early to rise, always professional, and never late for appointments. Her unexplained absence is a mystery to them and completely out of character."

"So apparently no known enemies lurking from the time they've known her. That makes the current task establishing Isabel's work routines, her expected patterns of comings and goings, any elements of her personal life known to her colleagues, and whether she had made any enemies at her time in Churchville. Would you agree?"

"We're on the same page."

Isabel's administrative assistant, Alice, was the first to be interviewed.

"For the record, our first interview begins with Alice Haywood. Ms. Haywood, you've already met Detective Rick Walker from York County, so we can dispense with introductions and get right to the point. Can you tell us about your relationship with Dr. Isabel Helms?"

"I've been her administrative assistant for a year now since she came to Churchville as the provost."

Rick took the lead. "Ms. Haywood, how would you describe that work relationship?"

"Isabel is the best boss I've ever known," Alice said, already fighting tears. "She makes me feel like a valued peer rather than just a secretary."

Rick continued, "Can you tell us what the daily routine in the office was like?"

"Dr. Helms is always in early. I get in around 8:30, and she's always here when I arrive. We start each day by going over times and arrangements for scheduled meetings, making sure our calendars are always coordinated. She's the most organized person I've ever worked with."

"Did you ever interact with her outside of work on a personal basis?"

"No, and I'm not sure why not. We certainly get along well at work. I think she just keeps work and personal life as two different things. She is very professional that way. It's never really come up."

"Did you ever know of her to have disagreements with anyone on campus?"

"I've been a senior staff administrator for fifteen years and witnessed all manner of disagreement, especially between faculty and staff. That's an unavoidable consequence of her job."

"Do you know of anyone that may harbor some ill will concerning the provost?"

"I don't think so, and I'll tell you why. This may be another part of Dr. Helm's remarkable ability to keep work and personal issues as two different things. She never holds a grudge. She treats everyone with extreme respect, and she never considers an uncomfortable incident as anything other than an incident.

"Do you understand what I'm saying? She is not judgmental about work disagreements. She does not consider anyone an enemy or adversary. She is truly thankful that others feel empowered to present challenging viewpoints, and she takes them seriously. No matter the outcome, arguments or altercations are not something she dwells on or seems to take personally. They are just more information, and she treats everyone as part of the solution. How could anyone hate her for that?"

Alice Haywood had an obvious love and affection for Isabel as a boss. She wasn't a suspect, and she wasn't being grilled, but the circumstances were so foreign that she broke down often.

Alice and the rest of the staff interviewed that day told a tale of a very steady, very gracious boss. She was described as accessible and sensitive to the people she worked with. Her routines at school were predictable and well-planned. She was on schedule, never flustered or mad, and always in control. Today's interviews yielded nothing new.

THURSDAY INTERVIEWS

E ven with an expedited "friends and family" handling of evidence at the state lab, DNA for Isabel Helms wouldn't be available any sooner than Sunday or Monday. It also wouldn't matter until and unless they had something to match it to. The fingerprint evidence had been processed, and samples matched Isabel's records from her employment files. The keys, contents of the purse, and the notes in the leather organizer proved unremarkable. The phone was an iPhone. Apple was notoriously reticent to allow any access to user data on these, but it was a school-supplied resource, so the IT folks already had full access. The content was the unremarkable expected ordinary records of business. The same was true for her school-supplied laptop. There was nothing of a personal or suggestive nature found on either of those devices.

As the interview net expanded, some possible clues and directions for further search surfaced. Universally, the administrative staff and directors liked Isabel and praised her competency and judgment. As they opened conversations with the faculty and general staff, an interesting pattern began to emerge for Detective Rick Walker. It was not a surprise for Don Weston. There seemed to be more cautious and guarded responses in these groups as opposed to the open love fest of the main administration building. Some gentle probing shed light on the perceived ranking of faculty, related fears, jealousies, and maybe even dislikes. Don, of course, had been aware of the changes in faculty favorites dating back to the previous dean. He was also aware of the ongoing "faculty appraisal" meetings, often ending in retirements or separations. Budgets and headcount were under intense scrutiny.

Don had not warned Rick about the environment of the general staff and faculty experiences. He wanted Rick's fresh perspective on this. Don knew his own leanings and bias on the decision-making of the past few years, and he didn't want that to color any potential questions or interpretations of answers. The true situation and its impact on individuals appeared to run even deeper than Don Weston realized. Don was now planning to take himself out of the interview loop and have a Pennsylvania state law-enforcement investigator join Rick. He'd finish out today and ask Lester Timmons to supply the state resource by Monday.

The various interviewees expressed dissatisfaction with the current direction of the university, and all were concerned about job security. Some of the group included professors already slated to end their careers on the last day of this semester. Their personal opinions of Isabel were mixed. Some saw her as cold and calculating, while others felt she was just following Harold Olson's direction. A few expressed that Isabel could have been concerned about her own job security.

They were going to wrap things up as much as they could today and postpone the next steps of the interview process to Monday. Friday would have been spotty anyway, as Spring Break commenced on Saturday. All students, faculty, and staff were off campus for the following week, and most left early on Friday. The Olsons would remain on campus during the break. Don already had much contact with them and wanted to hold their recorded interviews just over the weekend when Lester Timmon's detective resource would be present to team up with Rick Walker. It looked like Don Weston might make his Gettysburg trip after all, until an early afternoon interview with an adjunct professor changed the investigation direction completely.

Veronica "Ronnie" Taruta was a young English teacher, a little Goth and very direct in her demeanor. Her work status fell under the title of visiting professor, so she was in the group that had received their discharge notices several weeks ago. Don made the formal introductions, and Rick took the lead on questioning.

"Ms. Taruta," started Rick, only to be interrupted.

"Please call me Ronnie," she said.

"Okay, Ronnie, we're investigating the disappearance of Dr. Isabel Helms. Our primary interest at this point is to establish her routines in and out of school and attempt to surface any potential concerns that may relate to her absence. We have heard from some faculty members about recent personnel adjustments. Is that something you can tell us more about?"

"I guess you mean the purge? It's not been popular. I went to Churchville for my undergrad and came back here when I got my master's. I love the place and have a lot of friends in faculty and staff here from my school days. I thought my future was here, but suddenly it's not."

"One of the things we're trying to identify is what impact such changes are having for individual faculty members."

"Like would I want to kill her?"

"Would you?"

"Not hardly, I'd like to thank her. I had no idea how bad my pay was until I got canned and had to look around. I found a job at the community college a week later at double the pay and much better state benefits. I'll miss my friends here, but my financial future is improved."

"You have no hard feelings from the purge?"

"Why would I want to stay where I'm not wanted?"

"Makes sense," said Rick. "Do you know of anyone who may have had interaction with the provost outside of school hours?"

"Actually, I have. There's a writing and poetry group that meets monthly at a bookstore in Statler, Pennsylvania. Dr. Helms would show up there sometimes. She always came in at the last minute and sat at the back of the room, usually leaving early without talking to anyone. She never acknowledged me or any of my friends, which was fine. I took that as a 'separation of church and state' thing for her."

This was news and, except for local restaurant visits, the first glimpse of an off-campus, social persona for Isabel Helms.

"You never saw her interact with anyone else there?"

"No, but she was very focused on the presentations of the readings. She took a lot of notes on her iPad and sometimes a Moleskine journal. I'd heard she was a poet, like me, but we never had an occasion to compare notes."

Ronnie had no fears or concerns and no guarded responses, a good witness.

This became the last faculty interview for Thursday—and beyond, as it turned out. Rick and Don would be back at Isabel's house early the next morning, searching for an iPad and Moleskine journals.

GLENN WEAVER

One of the hardest hits in the faculty "purge" was Glenn Weaver, primarily for reasons unknown to anyone else. Glenn was an artist of renown in the small Churchville community and surrounding area. His pottery and sculpture could be found at many local businesses and entertainment venues. He was also an art instructor at Churchville University, until he suddenly wasn't.

The Glenn Weaver that everyone knew had been eroding for months. The long hair and unkempt work clothes were still present, but the easygoing, happy-go-lucky, quick-witted personality had faded into bouts of depression and searing headaches. He had become a shadow of his medium-sized Keebler elf image.

Glenn's parents, Michael and Sally, were genuine hippies, drawn to the San Francisco Bay area around the Summer of Love in 1967. He grew up puttering around his dad's art shop, helping customers, and throwing clay in between home schooling. Both parents also maintained an interest in organic farming.

Glenn was a solitary soul even then. He loved to disassemble and figure out how mechanical things worked. He also grew up with early computers. Glenn's parents gave him an official indoctrination into the finer points of dope smoking, starting on his thirteenth birthday. He had stolen the occasional joint before and puffed it in the woods like other kids did with their parents' cigarettes. He became an official taste tester for the harvests of the family farm.

Glenn got his education through an MFA at a local college while living and working at home. After that he wandered the country for a few years, looking for himself. Glenn had found his calling at Churchville University a thousand miles away, but the family remained bonded in love and closeness.

Glenn's artistic acceptance at Churchville allowed for his social acceptance as a quirky character. He was deemed to be brilliant, and the occasional synapse misfires from a lifetime of heavy THC exposure were just a part of who he was. He had the capacity for highly intellectual exchanges and engaged as necessary in his academic and art show times. He just preferred to eschew all politics and mindless chit-chat to live in the easy smiling and laughing nature that reflected the mellow, free-flowing space in his head. He tried to avoid angry thoughts. Suddenly those angry thoughts were unavoidable.

Glenn lived in the woods on a hundred-acre, mountainside forest sanctuary. The land was cheap as it was relatively worthless for any development, but it was perfect for his private mind. Glenn created an A-frame cottage for a home and added several outbuildings, including a large barn that was scheduled to be razed as a local farm was becoming a neighborhood. He moved it plank by plank and reconstructed it faithfully to its rustic heritage. This was his workshop. A barely navigable clearing of a road wound lazily through the woods, but once the electricity and gas hookups were in, he didn't favor random visitors in this space anyway.

He often sampled his drug of choice in a secluded clearing in the woods. There, he had constructed a quarter-scale model of "Foamhenge." In the center, he planted an expendable cannabis crop for the grazing pleasure of his fellow woodland creatures. He was complete and whole as an individual entity. He didn't need any external appraisal or approval to be what he was. It was unfortunate that changes beyond the forest could ever intrude on such inner peace, but a cancer diagnosis did just that.

An annoying cough led Glenn from the school nurse to an X-ray, to spots on his lungs, to an oncology specialist, to a biopsy, to a carcinoma of unknown, primary diagnosis, and to further tests. Glenn was never a guy who had headaches, but he had them now. He ascribed that symptom to the tension of current events and could often, but not always, put it to rest with the right dose of cannabis. The headaches also came with unexplained and undirected irritability. He was uncharacteristically yelling and cursing in his workshop, throwing pottery pieces and sculpture scraps for no reason.

He had managed all this privately through the first month of the school semester. His last visit confirmed the primary pancreatic cancer and his outlook, which was none. He suddenly had no job and no future on this Earth. They say you shouldn't back a man into a corner when he has nothing to lose. Glenn found unguided hate creeping up on him.

Glenn sat alone in his thoughts Tuesday morning while he created and uncreated the clay spinning on the pottery wheel in his quiet barn. There had been some faculty gossip and rumors over the past month or so at Churchville about the pending "faculty assessment" meetings with the provost. Glenn, as usual, paid no attention to the political grumblings, happy in his own gig, still troubled by the recent medical revelation that life was short.

He was genuinely surprised when his provost meeting was over, along with his career. There was no net when he fell from the high wire in his head. "Thanks, I understand," was all he could muster before he left the conference room. He didn't have any classes that day, so he drove through the beautiful countryside for hours, smoking a joint, intermittently singing to the tunes from the mp3 player, and breaking down in tears.

The day after his firing notice, Glenn was setting up a scheduled art show at York County Community College. He had an unexpected visitor there and a chance to share some of his grief. Dr. James Giles used to drop in on Glenn's art shows when Giles was the dean at Churchville. Glenn was surprised to see him. Their relationship had always been purely administrative school contact, but it was different now.

Glenn watched James park and walk up. He dropped a pitchfork-haired, metal face back into the truck and met James halfway with a sincere hug. Heaving sobs with floods of tears running off his wild mustache, he said, "James, they fired me."

"I heard that," said Giles.

Glenn also shared his cancer diagnosis, laying bare the hopeless, helpless outlook of life after Churchville. "James," said Glenn. "I'm angry. Angry at cancer, angry at God, angry that I'll never see my parents again, angry that my work no longer means anything, and angry at Harold Olson and Isabel Helms."

"They're not good people," said Giles. "They're destroying the school and destroying lives. Maybe we can destroy them," he whispered, part statement, part question.

That was three weeks ago.

BACK TO TODAY

Glenn and Harold

Glenn's course load consisted of two classes on Tuesday and two on Thursday. On both days, class times were 2:00 p.m. and 5:00 p.m. The early ones were clay pottery, and the evening sessions were metal sculpture this semester. It wasn't unusual to see Glenn puttering about the campus on class days. Many of the large student welding projects took place outside in various locations. It was normal that he would be carrying pieces of angle iron about, probably positioning some inventory for yet more sculpture.

When Glenn was making his rounds on Thursday, he swung by the president's office. Harold was in and allowed a visit.

"Thanks for seeing me," Glenn said.

"I'm glad to see you," responded Harold. "I have a lot of respect and appreciation for your art and how you've brought it to the campus through your students. I regret that our last meeting was our first meeting. It wasn't the kind of introduction I would have preferred us to have."

"I understand the position the college is in and the hard decisions you have to make. I want you to know I can accept the pending separation without hardship and support myself just fine in the art business."

"That's good to know. These changes are quite painful for everyone involved." Harold's guard was down from that point. "What can I do for you?"

Glenn's headache was splitting his skull, and his recently emergent anxiety, confusion, and hatred were threatening to explode with it. Glenn focused intensely on presenting a neutral conversation. He had an important message to deliver.

"I wanted to fill you in on a facility issue. In my work with the drama folks, I noticed something of concern in the auditorium. It has to do with a potential structural issue in a wall and the roof supports. It appears to be stable now, but if it progressed, it would present a costly inspection and possibly reconstruction to shore it up. My reason for coming to you directly is to keep it low key and not raise any drama from students or faculty about the use of the facility and adjoining buildings if it never got worse. Some activities are using the auditorium today, but I know it will be empty after noon tomorrow, so that might be the best time to check it out."

Expenses were always on Harold's mind. The last thing he needed was another major, unplanned expense and additional outside focus on an aging, overtaxed infrastructure. Harold and Glenn agreed that it should be investigated quickly and quietly while Glenn was still on board. They would keep it between the two of them at this point. Harold's calendar was open after 3:00 p.m. Friday. Glenn had a previous engagement that he couldn't break, but he told the president exactly how to see the object of concern.

"Dr. Olson, if you enter the auditorium and go to center stage, just beyond the main curtain, you'll be able to see what I've seen. Look straight up past the stage lighting rails, and you'll find the crack in the roof. If it's not overcast, you may even be able to see some light filtering in from outside. It's a concern for sure, but hopefully one that can be easily addressed."

The auditorium was on the way from Harold's office, so Harold would stroll by after 3:00 p.m. on his walk home tomorrow afternoon to check things out. Glenn reiterated that he thought that was a good plan, thanked him, and left. Glenn desperately needed to medicate his head before he burst.

Harold hated surprises, but this one was possibly not a problem and might be easily correctable. It was just one more executive task to determine, and a diversion might be welcome. The diversion he needed was anything to get his mind redirected from the one thing that trumped financial concerns: the missing Isabel.

Harold already knew about Don Weston's plans for tomorrow and Monday and that further feedback from the state lab was not imminently expected. A late afternoon walk might be a nice transition to the weekend. The campus would be empty by then for Spring Break, so he shouldn't be held up in his walk by anyone or anything else. With any luck, Glenn's concerns would turn out to be overly cautious and something that could be watched or easily patched up.

A SECOND SEARCH

On Friday morning, Don Weston and Rick Walker met at the home of Isabel Helms. They were joined there by an evidence technician from the Pennsylvania state lab. The Ronnie Taruta revelation that Isabel Helms "took a lot of notes on her iPad and sometimes a Moleskine journal" was the prime focus of their visit. Don broke his seal on the front door, unlocked it with Elly's key, and the three men entered. Everyone wore gloves.

Since the scene was new to the evidence tech, Don reviewed what had been found and taken during the first search. He shared the evidence pictures and images showing the items in place before they were bagged and tagged. Don suggested that Rick join the evidence tech, letting him go over all the rooms and remaining items to see everything with fresh eyes. While they were walking through the small house, Don checked the rest of his seals on the other house doors, the Prius, and the detached garage. All were intact. Don was curious about the old wardrobe cabinet in the garage, but they would not be entering the garage or opening the cabinet today.

Don was very careful and clear on the purpose of the search and evidence. By the doctrine of exigent circumstances, he could support their first official search in a court of law. Technically, that right expired when they found no body or evidence of a crime. They were already on shaky legal ground with their second entry. If they found the iPad, he didn't doubt they would be secure there as well. Beyond that, without clear evidence of foul play or a crime having been committed, they had no grounds to break into a locked cabinet or remove anything else. The last thing Don wanted was to find a real crime scene elsewhere and then lose any potential evidence from this one on a technical gaffe.

Don now turned to the library nook. There were a lot of reference books, poetry books, a scattering of popular novels, and a shelf of Moleskine journals. Still gloved, he started perusing the contents of the bookshelf. Don kept journals on his Civil War research and field experience and was respectful that he might be entering a very private space. If he found anything in the way of clues in these books, he would likely not admit to touching them and pursue a search warrant on other grounds for these and the contents of the garage.

As it turned out, many of the journals were empty, just waiting for their time on the shelf. In the ones with content, he was impressed with Dr. Helms' organization, discipline, and readable penmanship. Isabel had well-practiced, classical cursive handwriting. In his cursory examination, Don found no potential evidence here. The active notebooks served different purposes. Isabel practiced multiple poetic styles such as sonnets, haiku, and even limericks, seemingly as exercise. She also captured thought starters in her books. These were likely the journals that joined her at the poetry readings. There were no diaries and no secrets.

Rick Walker and the state evidence tech completed their search of the three small rooms in the house.

"Don," Rick said. "We've found nothing new in the other rooms. How are you doing here?"

"Same, no iPad and nothing out of the ordinary in her journals."

It appeared the possessions already in evidence would be it. The evidence tech expressed specific interest in the office area of the great room. He asked, "Would it be appropriate for me to attempt access to this laptop on the docking station?"

"Not necessary," said Don. "That unit is school property. The school IT department and I have already been through it with no useful results."

The three men regrouped in the front yard after Don had affixed a new seal on the house. There was no iPad found. There was also no evidence of more than an adult missing person, no seeming crime scene, and no overt signs of foul play. Don would see Rick on

Monday morning when Rick would be joined by the second detective interviewer from the state. They all went on to their weekends.

Don Weston returned to his campus office. He sent emails to his initial police contacts and Harold Olson. These were a top-line recap of the week's events. The police ones had some additional technical details relating to search-and-seizure protocol, but they were all brief, just courtesy correspondence and reiteration of the pending Monday interviews for Harold and Elly. Don hopped into his car, which was already packed, and pointed it to Gettysburg. He wouldn't be making the Antietam/Shenandoah tour next week, but he could escape the current concerns and wallow in the epitome of civil war-ness from this moment until Monday morning.

GLENN'S FRIDAY

Glenn's Friday morning started the usual way. He headed to the barn to throw some clay and smoke a joint. This morning's choice was rolled with an especially potent blend from his mother's crop. She was much on his mind. Glenn inhaled the couple of drags that induced a balanced buzz and set the rest aside. He had plans to smoke the entire joint that evening when his day was done. He was already looking forward to a long, long nap.

When he finished puttering, he returned to the house, looked at the computer screen, and cried. He was in fear and a bubbling rage, alone in his head and alone in his soul. He had planned a preemptive strike on his soon-pending helplessness and imminent doom. Today had been his last sunrise, and tonight would be his final sunset.

Now, he typed:

Dear Mom and Dad,

> *When you read these words, I'll be gone. Please don't grieve. You have given me all the love and freedom that a man could hope for in life, and I hope you can understand why I've made the choices I have.*
>
> *I couldn't tell you about a terminal cancer diagnosis because I couldn't stand to hurt you so badly twice. You would have to watch the wasting of your only son, and his ultimate death. I know this note will be hard on you, but I'm exiting your lives now only once, and only in love.*

Mariposa and my little plot here are the only homes I've ever known, and I choose this one for my tranquil exit. Be at peace that it will be a relatively quick and painless end. The only alternative was neither.

I've not been a religious man, but you raised me with a spiritual sense. I trust we'll enjoy each other's company again. Per Rumi:

> *"Out beyond ideas of wrongdoing*
> *and rightdoing there is a field*
> *I'll meet you there*
> *When the soul lies down in that grass*
> *the world is too full to talk about"*

Your loving son, Glenn
p.s. – Thank you James for being a friend at the end

Glenn Weaver's last recorded thoughts would be found in print on his kitchen table. He left home that morning, dressed in his workshop clothes, got into his old pickup, ground the manual gears, and rolled down the mountain to Churchville. He'd have a few hours of creative time alone.

THIS ONE THEY'LL FIND

The only sound was the soft hiss and pop of the welder as bars of thick angle iron were sealed to the outside edges of the steel fire door. This was the final step before walking away, as every other door of the building had already been secured with the same treatment from the inside. The technician was satisfied with the afternoon's work.

The edifice just secured was the auditorium on the campus of Churchville University. The school was going on break. The campus was virtually empty and would be for another week. The next time someone entered this hall would be after a significant effort of demolition to overcome the welder's work, unlikely to be a priority for a while, as there were no scheduled events for weeks.

Inside the seating area of the auditorium, all was dark; the heavy, black, velvet drapes of the theatrical curtain were drawn. Behind the curtain, the hot, bright stage lights were burning at full wattage, unseen except if one was on the boards of the stage. And one was.

The silent performance was that of one man. He was naked, his head awkwardly shaved with large tufts of hair still hanging on as if he had been exposed to the poisonous ravages of chemotherapy or scalped by some deranged Edward Scissorhands. There was a ball gag stuffed in his mouth, secured by a heavy leather strap buckled tightly against the back of his crown. The apparatus was wrapped in further layers of duct tape, ensuring that the last sounds of his life were already history. He was also tightly zip-tied at his wrists and ankles, hands behind his back.

The set for tonight's performance was a raised hydraulic platform that was leaking fluid from a hose at its base. The man knelt atop the monument in an odd, crouched position, both supported and tortured by an intricate harness of rope and wires. The detail was exquisite in design and function.

Tucked deeply into the crack of his anus, and tied tightly around his testicles, was a large, garish bow tie. Threaded through the fabric, a thin but very sturdy loop of razor wire encircled the base of the scrotum. A relatively short, heavy gauge cable was attached to the razor wire and extended tightly up the man's torso where it was secured at the base of a noose surrounding his neck, hence the uncomfortable crouch. The noose was tied off in the rafters of the stage with only inches of slack before it would increasingly tighten as the hydraulic fluid drained out and the platform slowly sank.

The prisoner's dilemma allowed for some choices. As his supporting base dropped, the noose would begin to restrict his airflow. The first choice was that he could, and likely would, lift his head in a basic survival instinct to ward off the airway obstruction. Choice two, lifting his head further, would draw the razor wire against, and eventually through, the silk fabric of his penile adornment and through the soft skin of his formerly proud manhood.

A third choice would be to force oneself off the tower. This would accomplish both ends, leaving a coroner to determine if the cause of death was asphyxiation from the noose or exsanguination from the removal of the genitals. Whether or not the man chose the boldest of options, the result would ultimately be the same. And this all would take place slowly at first, then, with a sudden grand finale in total silence on the lit stage with the performer as his only audience.

The man's eyes alternated between tightly closed, leaking tears of pain and frustration, to wildly and inhumanly open, a picture of sheer horror. He might have been a handsome man once, but you'd never know that now, overshadowed by his new haircut, his kneeling squat, and the mimed expressions of agony, muffled by his mouth harness. His shins and knees were fading into complete numbness after already enduring a seemingly endless twenty minutes of awkward kneeling.

There would be a puddle of hydraulic fluid remaining when he was found. There would also be a large, corresponding stain from the release of all his intestinal contents and bodily fluids: blood, sweat, and tears.

THE END OF THE BARN AT THE HUNDRED-ACRE WOODS

At 6:00 p.m. on Friday, the start of Spring Break for Churchville University, it was time for Glenn to go home, forever.

Glenn pulled the little brass pipe and the torch lighter from his console. He had made the pipe about thirty years ago. It was constructed of fittings he matched from a cabinet of brass hardware in an auto parts store. He was especially fond of the screw-off cap that let him load it up, burn what he wanted at one time, and store the rest for the next use. He usually loaded it on Monday mornings, and the contents took him through the full week of commuting. He took the long, pretty route home today, which was very pleasant and peaceful. Hank Williams serenaded the scenery.

When he had cleared the Baja of a driveway, he went to the house first. Glenn had meticulously visualized every step of the next hour. His mental dress rehearsal was now a real performance with no audience. In the house, he went directly to the "wine cellar." He selected ten mason jars of the finest aged herbs and loaded them into a couple of reusable Aldi bags from the kitchen. He'd miss Aldi. They had the greatest prices on the charcuterie snacks of meat and cheese that made up his favorite munchies. While in the kitchen he purposely avoided looking at the note on the table. That scene of the play was already over.

The two weighty bags of glass containers accompanied him to the barn, clanking merrily along the way. Glenn was feeling mischievous from his little buzz on the ride home. He grandly opened the big barn doors and yelled, "Here's Johnny!" into the empty cavern.

The next task began the descent into hell with fire and brimstone. He fired up all three of his traditional wood- and coal-stoked pottery kilns. He also had one modern, gas-fired kiln and cranked open the valve. He had piped gas ignitors to all and usually kept them at least warm. Today, he filled their respective fuel chambers and let them start climbing to their terminal temperatures. The single giant wood stove for heating the barn was also packed with fuel and now sucking oxygen. Glenn always had large wooden crates filled with kindling and coal at each of the vintage furnaces. As the heat was building, he lit the joint he had left there this morning for some glorious refreshment. His head would be in the right spot when the curtain fell on this performance.

A few years back Glenn had rented a booth at a local town fair to display and sell some pottery and other small art pieces. The booth setting up next to him attracted his "mechanical thing" radar, and he struck up a conversation with the petite vendor. She was a franchisee for Damsels in Defense, a product line of self-defense items for women.

The array of products was fascinating to Glenn, especially the prominently displayed and billed "handheld nightmare" of a stun baton. It was said to be a delivery device of 600,000 volts of deterrence and/or submission to a presumed giant of a male attacker. Glenn found himself giggling throughout the day every time he jumped at the powerful crackling of the baton being demonstrated. In between alternating crushes and droughts of customers, the two vendors chatted. At the end of the day when packing up, Glenn gifted the Damsel a piece of metal sculpture in exchange for a wand of his own.

In addition to just being a cool toy and "mechanical thing," the baton was to have a practical purpose. The hundred-acre woods of Glenn's compound were also home to a variety of visitors, from squirrels to deer to foxes and even bears. The sound of the crackle alone sent all matter of critters quickly scurrying. He tucked it into the hammer loop of his coveralls when he was on a walkabout between his buildings. It was there today. He pulled the gift of the Damsel from the hammer loop of his coveralls and gave it one last burst of frightening energy as he cracked himself up with his best Dorothy imitation: "I'll miss you most of all, 'Scare' crow." He tossed it in the big wood stove, along with his cell phone.

He took intermittent drags from his stout, hand-rolled doobie as he followed the remaining steps of the script. "Pace yourself Glenny-boy, the best is yet to come," he said aloud. Some of the contents from the coal pile and the kindling bins were now distributed along the outer walls of the barn and in piles at the feet of the wooden columns that supported the massive beams. He wandered the distribution path a second time, adding fire from a hand-held torch to the little stacks of fuel. As the kindling and coal began to slowly flicker, Glenn closed the giant door for the last time.

Now for the climax. Returning to the big wood stove, he bashed it mightily in the throat of its exhaust pipe with a small sledgehammer, the broken plumbing now allowing smoke to escape within the building. The Aldi bags were emptied and tossed in the flames along with all the contents of the mason jars from the "wine cellar." Glenn closed the flue some, maximizing the output of the cannabis smoke filling the room. Perfect!

The protagonist now sat cross-legged on the dirt floor in the middle of the barn and surveyed his work. Small flames were growing larger all around him as they lapped at the walls of old wood. The precious kilns were performing their work to their full potential, sans their diet of clay. The finest-ever clouds of activated cannabis filled the air as Glenn sucked the last of his premium joint and ate the hot roach. The peace he craved was on its way. Glenn Weaver was as high as he had ever been. He lay on the dirt floor in the middle of his beloved shop, barely conscious and exquisitely stoned.

GETTYSBURG

Stonewall Jackson and Turner Ashby were on the porch, smoking cigars, when Don Weston drove up. Never mind that neither lived to fight at Gettysburg; this gathering was a time for amateur Civil War historians to immerse in history and speculation. Two of Don's old friends were just lounging in their reenactor garb for some upcoming Shenandoah Valley events.

Still, seeing the two Civil War figures together, in this place, played into one of the larger speculations about Gettysburg. Ashby was Jackson's brilliant cavalry lead in much of the Shenandoah Valley activity during the war. He was, unfortunately, lost to Stonewall when he was killed in an insignificant skirmish in Harrisonburg in 1862. Jackson himself succumbed to injury from friendly fire just after the Chancellorsville battle in May of 1863, before the history at Gettysburg. To this day there is lively debate among amateur historians and reenactors about how the Gettysburg outcome would have been different if these two men had been present there in early July of 1863.

The drive from Churchville was only an hour on the direct route. Civil War buffs take three or more hours following various battle campaigns and infantry movement routes. Don was anxious to get there but still wandered on and off Route 30 byways of interest. It was a good, mind-cleansing break. Let the banter begin.

Stonewall Jackson said, "What's the password so we know you're not some carpet bagger?"

Don responded, "Spangler Springs." The password was always Spangler Springs at Gettysburg. The Confederates dropped their guard to let him in. There was already a small camp set up in the yard with a few serious reenactors starting their weekend in character. Don had played a role there for the first couple of years with the group. He was still with the Philadelphia Police Department at the time and loved that total break from present to past. He'd since morphed into a senior historian position but still did inspections of the encampment. The men there would require further vetting to let him join that circle. It was 1863 in that part of the yard, and the camp was wary of strangers.

Don dropped his small bag on the porch and pulled up a rocking chair to join Jackson and Ashby. Another cigar and a ginger beer appeared to complete the welcome. It was 1863 in the yard but the present day on the porch.

"What's up, Captain?" asked the faux Stonewall Jackson.

"More than I'd like, I must pass on the Shenandoah Valley trip next week. Unfortunately, we have a missing person case going on at the college, and I'll need to be back there Monday."

Jackson and Ashby were also retired from the Philadelphia Police Department.

"Now, how the hell does that happen?" said Turner Ashby.

"Hard to say," Don responded. "It's a senior administrator who's been missing since Monday morning. If it was a student, I'd vote for an early Spring Break getaway, but this lady was in the middle of serious business for the week and just failed to post."

Jackson suggested, "Foul play perhaps?"

"No definitive sign of it. We searched her home twice. I already have state and local involved, and we sent some personal belongings to Harrisburg for DNA testing. No foreign fingerprints were found. Only her phone and one other item are known to be missing, but it's her personal iPad, so it could be significant."

Ashby said, "Well, good luck on that one."

"By the way," said Don to Jackson. "Kudos on scoring that factory-cased Beaumont-Adams sidearm for your Stonewall wear. That must have set you back close to five grand for correctness."

"It did," said Stonewall. "But go big or go home would have been the Stonewall battle approach, so it had to be. And here I sit period correct, which makes you look silly with that Colt 1911 you're wearing."

"I'm surprised the wife didn't choke on that investment."

"I buried it under 'car parts' for her '57 Thunderbird, so she's happy. What she doesn't know won't kill me."

At 6:00 p.m., while the boys were gathering and the tomfoolery was just beginning, Don got a text from Elly. "Harry is missing."

He didn't have another drive in him today, so he called and let her know he'd be back by 10:00 a.m. He'd missed out on the vacation trip next week, and now the entire boy's weekend and the ceremonial Pickett's Charge walk would be lost, too. He also called Rick Walker and told him to meet him at the office at 7:00 a.m. They'd be going back to video review in the morning, looking for the lost Harold Olson.

FIRE ON THE MOUNTAIN

The first fire call came in at 7:35 p.m. for smoke on the wooded mountain on the outskirts of Churchville. Several other 911 calls quickly followed, and a truck was dispatched. They had no exact address or coordinates. The fire chief didn't yet know what exactly was burning, but it appeared to be deep in the woods. He called the nearby Forest Service office and requested assistance. The Forest Service had specialized equipment that could better access wooded terrain.

It was after 8:00 p.m. before the general site was identified and almost 8:45 before potential access was found. The fire truck managed about half a mile up the rutted road, which just wasn't made for traffic. The crew ran ahead on foot to see what they were dealing with. One of the firefighters sprinted to the house to check for occupants as the rest of the team went directly to the fire site. They all noted the unusual smell of this fire, as a strong whiff of cannabis threatened a contact high.

What they found was a barn structure, fully involved in flames at this point. Fortunately, the wind was nonexistent, and the area around the structure was clear. The fire was burning vertically with little in the way of flying sparks to further endanger the nearby house, outbuildings, or the forest itself. They dropped fifteen hundred feet of hose from the pumper truck. It wouldn't reach the barn, but they were able to shoot some spray to the ground between the barn and the house for containment. With no other available resources, all they could do was watch the building burn.

Minutes after 9:00, with coordinates for the fire now established, two Forest Service 4WD jeeps with tanks arrived on the burn site. The building had just fallen in on itself. All hands attacked the embers and loose pieces from the building collapse with shovels and the limited water from the Jeeps. It became apparent that there was an operating ignition source within the barn. The firefighters discovered, and turned off, the gas feed for the kilns. The area outside of the barn footprint was rendered safe from expansion, and more Forest Service vehicles were on the way as the fire settled in place in its pile of depleting fuel.

By 10:30, additional Forest Service resources had arrived, and the crews began soaking the remains. A second pumper was already in place at the bottom of the drive to refill the Jeeps' smaller tanks as needed. By midnight, the structure was fully burned or soaked with only small wisps of occasional smoke present. Fire inspectors and local county police investigators were beginning to arrive at the scene.

No occupants were present in the house, outbuildings, or surrounding clearings. That was a concern, as there was a vehicle parked at the house. A second concern was the live gas feed to the barn. Was it possible that someone was in there working when the fire started? It would be several more hours before it was safe to start dragging the ashes for evidence of cause. The county police investigators moved to the house and other buildings.

Police had already done a property deed search and determined this was the residence of Glenn Weaver. In the residence, they found the suicide note on the kitchen table and began necessary precautions to secure the entire area as a crime scene. York County Sheriff Bill Hester got a 1:00 a.m. wakeup call with that news. "Keep me posted," Hester responded.

At 1:30 a.m., Hester was informed by one of his deputies that a check had been found. It was from Churchville University and noted as expense reimbursement to Glenn Weaver, a likely clue of employment. They told the sheriff they would follow up on that Monday morning. He told them he was already on it.

HEADING BACK TO CHURCHVILLE

Don Weston had a restless night in Gettysburg. The guys hung out on the porch and visited the encampment a couple of times that night, but the time was all too short, and he had too much on his mind. Don was up at 5:00 a.m. A voicemail from Bill Hester had come in at 1:30 that morning about the fire and suicide note at Glenn Weaver's home.

In the car at 6:00 a.m., Weston called Hester. Bill had stayed up, waiting for the response. Police and fire investigators were only now able to start clearing the barn scene but had already seen what appeared to be the classic fetal position of burned human remains. Don filled Bill in on the missing-person message from last night about Harold Olson. The two men briefly discussed the situation of two missing persons and a suicide connected to Churchville University in one week as likely more than a coincidence. Don let Hester know his previous plan to start reviewing security camera data when he got to the office. Hester let Don know he'd have the fire site under his care and Don should follow his existing plan.

After he hung up on the Hester call, Don spoke out loud alone in the car.

"Helen," he chuckled. "I think the action I thought I wanted has emerged."

Be careful what you ask for, whispered Helen.

"You're right, as always. What started as a simple missing person, expected to show up at any moment, seems to be turning into a shit-storm of a puzzle."

You're good at puzzles, you always find the missing pieces.

"I don't know, Helen; I can't even find the border pieces on this one yet."

You will, Don, you will. I'm here for you if you need me. Love you.

Don made another call to his old friend, Darell Metz.

"What's up, Chief?" Darrel answered.

"I'm driving back to campus from my Gettysburg trip. Just needed to hear the voice of an old cop friend. What's up with you?"

"Retirement planning. Still have a couple of years to go but I've decided to pursue an MBA to up my next career prospects. I need a couple of business prerequisites, so next year I'll be back in school at the local community college to polish those off."

"I'm still thinking about another retirement myself. Maybe you should take this job."

"Really? You didn't make it sound so politically attractive the last time we talked," laughed Darell. "Can you throw in some used Kleenex or toilet paper to sweeten the deal?" More laughter.

Don laughed with him. He needed some levity before he went on.

"Darell, do you remember last year when we checked out Churchville's pending president and provost?"

"How could I forget Log Cabin ribeye, oatmeal raisin cookies, and Zerbe's chips? I thought you guys hired them. How's that been going?"

"Pretty well up until now. I've spent time since then with the president and his wife and done many campus events with them and the provost, absolute professionals. I've been enjoying their company. Harold's wife, Elly, even asked me to do a background check on one of their daughter's prospective boyfriends."

"How did that go?"

"Fine, your basic frat boy lacrosse player, nothing sinister. Probably a perfect fit for the family," Don chuckled. "I was arriving at a mindset that our suspicions from the vetting process were just coincidences."

"Until?"

Serious now. "The provost became a missing person on Monday. No one has seen or heard from her all week."

"Hmmmm."

"It gets better. The president became a missing person last night."

"Think they've run off together?"

"I doubt it. I have some suspicion of foul play in the provost's disappearance."

"Maybe all the more reason for the president to disappear," laughed Darell.

"Now that I've come to know and like these people, I think I'd prefer if they had run off together, but I'm pretty sure that's not the happy ending we're going to find. There's more in the developing story."

"What's that?"

We also had a major fire at a faculty member's home last night. They may have a body, but we can't verify it's him yet. He left a suicide note."

"Is that related?"

"Too soon to tell, but I can't help assuming it will be. Three missing people in one week from the same small community is odd and suspicious indeed."

"You're really sweetening the pot now. I see an unlimited supply of used Kleenex and toilet paper in your immediate future."

"Well, I'm getting close to school, so I should probably sign off for now. This morning will be a security tape review with the Sheriff's Department. I did need to hear a friendly voice, and you've provided just that."

"Keep me posted. I see another road trip and a hearty Don Weston meal in the aftermath of your adventure." One last laugh for both of them.

SHOWTIME

Weston took the direct route to the office, getting there at 7:00 a.m. A pot of coffee and a campus video review would start the work weekend that Saturday. Rick Walker arrived as the coffee was poured. They discussed the coincidence of last night's fire. They felt in their guts there had to be some connection to the other campus disappearances, but, evidentially, that remained to be seen. Don told him to get comfortable while the chief was getting started on the new video search for Dr. Harold Olson. Don thought about Glenn Weaver. He was a weird little leprechaun of an art guy, always fun to run into on campus. It was sad news, indeed, if he was gone.

By 8:00, Don had what he needed. Harold Olson had left his office at 2:33 p.m. Friday. He meandered a bit, crossing campus. He was on camera entering the new library building. He was also seen leaving ten minutes later. A stroll across the main lawn had him heading into the Student Union by 3:00. The Student Union building is connected to many things. There were academic offices there for Family and Consumer Sciences along with the Art Department classes and labs. He didn't head in that direction. He headed to his right, past the cafeteria, and onto the assembly room area of the building. He was last picked up entering the auditorium at 3:07 p.m.

Rick was refilling their coffee and watching over Don's shoulder as he switched to the interior auditorium camera and the next images appeared. Harold Olson was seen purposefully walking through the seating area and climbing the stairs to the stage. The curtains were open, and the stage lighting was oddly on. Harry walked through the opening and looked up at the ceiling, craning his neck and shielding his eyes from the stage lighting, intently focusing on something in the air.

"What's that?" Rick asked the chief. A figure in black was emerging like a shadow against the front of the stage curtain. Rick and Don Weston watched as the shadow crept up behind the president, delivered a thundering kick from behind to Olson's groin, and quickly jumped on the injured victim to tie wrap his ankles and hands.

"This was yesterday," said Don. "We can watch the video later; we need to go now!"

Rick was already headed to the door when Don said, "Wait, I want to take a look at the current footage from that camera." The new picture was an empty auditorium with curtains drawn. The two men sprinted across the campus.

The auditorium main doors didn't even have a lock. There was a lobby at the entryway that could be secured, but it never was. Anyone on campus could walk into the lecture hall any time of day or night. But not today. Don and Rick were not small guys, but the large, previously unsecured entry doors wouldn't budge. A quick run around the building confirmed all the other metal doors were equally inaccessible. The main wood doors opened from the outside in, so no hinges were exposed. Don called local fire and rescue and told them to bring a Hannigan bar and an axe. It would be a shame to damage these old doors, but they were going to be opened soon, one way or another.

A team from fire and rescue was on the scene by 10:00 a.m. By 10:30, the Hannigan tool had made some splinters but failed to breach the doors. The axe was not much more effective; the doors were too solid and too thick. The doors were mightily damaged but no less secure. Don Weston assured the team there were no concerns about damage at this point as they were standing at the last-known sighting of the university president who had been reported missing roughly fifteen hours ago. A chainsaw was the next choice.

While the team was gathering new tools, Don Weston inquired if anyone had been working the fire in the woods last night. One of the firefighters answered, "I just came from there. I'm still on call from last night."

"How was it?"

"A virtually inaccessible spot deep in the woods. There was a large barn fully engulfed in flames. We were able to get Forest Service vehicles in to stop the fire from spreading to the house or other buildings. Fortunately, the area around the barn was well-cleared. Except for that, we would have lost everything and been dealing with a full-scale forest fire now. Everything at that site was in control when I left."

"Sheriff Hester told me there may have been human remains there."

"We were able to see a possible body in the center of the scene, but it's going to take more time for things to cool off before that can be verified, which I think it will be. The darndest thing about the whole scene was the smoke. Instead of the expected acrid smell, we were buried in a cloud of what I would swear was cannabis burning. It was more like being at Woodstock than at a fire scene."

The conversation was interrupted by the sounds of the demolition on the door. The saw bit into the center gap that had been widened with the Hannigan and the axe. The wood was now giving up to the carbon-tipped chain when it violently kicked back, having struck something more solid. The firefighter tried another direction, finding success again until another intense interruption was encountered. Working the middle ground, they eventually opened a hole big enough for one of the firefighters to get his head inside. He could see where the angle-iron frame that was holding the door was attached. A man-sized hole was opened on the lower part of the door by noon. Don and Rick asked the firefighters to stay behind and keep the opening secure. Then, they crawled through a very tight squeeze for the six-foot-five Weston.

After examining the reinforcement structure on the inside of the auditorium doors, the two men walked cautiously down the main aisle. Nothing seemed out of place or unusual. As they got closer to the stage area, there was a whiff of sewage in the air. This was not uncommon in the basements of the overcrowded dorm buildings, but Don didn't recall ever smelling it here. When Don Weston pulled back the center of the stage curtain, the smell was intense, coupled with a blast of heat from the burning lights. The scene behind the curtain was gruesome. The body of President Harold Olson faced them, eyes open, hanging by his neck at center stage, unquestionably dead.

Don and Rick took phone pictures and made observations from the apron of the stage. They would not enter further or risk changing anything until the coroner and the crime-scene investigators arrived from the Harrisburg State Police lab. They noted the body was nude. The head was partially shaved, and clumps of hair were on the floor below the hanging body. There was duct tape around the head. As they had already witnessed, there were zip ties at the ankles and wrists with the hands secured behind his back.

The neck did not appear to be broken. There was a substantial wound in the genital area where the man's scrotum and penis appeared to have been severed. A large quantity of bodily fluids—excrement, possibly urine, and blood—was present. These fluids were on the deck of a platform lift parked directly below the body and spattered from there to the floor of the stage. They also noted the intense heat from the stage lighting. The hydraulic platform lift was almost completely descended to a park position, and hydraulic fluid appeared to have leaked from one of the hoses on the piece of equipment.

Don called the County Sheriff and Colonel Lester Timmons' office. The Pennsylvania State Police Bureau of Criminal Investigation and the coroner would be on the scene in a few hours. County police were there in minutes to man the outside of the auditorium 24/7 until all investigation was completed. They left the now-secured murder site and moved to join the current investigation at Glenn Weaver's house. They had plenty of evidence to pursue now.

When they got to Glenn Weaver's house at 2:30 p.m., fire and county investigators were on the scene. Don, Rick, and the county sheriff agreed that this location would also wait for the state coroner and state crime lab technicians before further work was done. Don took a picture with his phone of the suicide note, still on the kitchen table. He also took pictures of the general scene and what appeared to be a charred body in the center of the barn area.

Don spent another twenty minutes walking around the rest of the property and the rutted driveway. By the side of the road, a bit more than halfway to the house, he saw a large chunk of what appeared to be a vehicle taillight lens near the road. Probably nothing, he thought, but he picked it up and took it with him. They went back to Churchville University to inform the president's wife that he was deceased.

CHAPLAIN ON BOARD

Ethan McCallum was the university chaplain; Don called him from Glenn's house and was fortunate enough to find him on campus and available. Don wanted Ethan to join him and Rick to see Elly Olson. Ethan was a peaceful, soft-spoken, naturally empathetic human being, and his presence would be good for all. Don shared with Ethan that it appeared to be a murder. He also filled him in on the possible suicide of Glenn Weaver. Coupled with the missing Isabel Helms, the Churchville campus would need a chaplain more than ever in the coming days. Don knew Ethan as a safe confidant, and he thought some more detail would help Ethan prepare for their visit.

"Well?" said a smiling Elly Olson as she answered the door to the three men. Elly was an optimist and fully expected that Harold and Isabel were cooking up some exquisite surprise for her. She turned ashen when she realized that Ethan McCallum was part of the group.

"Elly," said Don. "This is Detective Rick Walker from the county sheriff's office. Maybe we can sit in the living room to talk?"

Elly sat on the couch, and Ethan joined her there. Don and Rick sat on the edge of their chairs facing her. Don Weston was very direct in what he said next. "Elly, Harold is no longer missing. He's dead."

For long seconds, she didn't seem to hear or comprehend the message. Ethan took her hand as she began to cry. "What happened? How?" she asked.

Don continued, "It appears he was murdered."

"That's not possible," she said, regaining some composure. "We talked after lunch yesterday, and he said he was coming home early.

That's why I messaged you last night when he wasn't here by 6:00. Where was he? What happened?" She broke down again.

"We found his body in the auditorium. The medical examiner will be here shortly, and we'll know more soon. I promise we'll keep you informed."

"I want to see him."

"Elly, I know, but that's not possible right now. The Pennsylvania State Police Bureau of Criminal Investigation is taking charge of the scene and the next steps. Even I can't see him until the crime scene is documented and cleared, which I expect will be much later tonight."

"An autopsy will be done to determine the exact cause of his death," Don continued. "I'll ask the medical examiner if you can see him before he is transported."

"Oh, my God, I'll have to call the kids. What will I say?"

"Ethan will be with you if you need him. I suggest you also gather any other close friends who can help right now."

"My two best friends are Harry and Isabel, and I can't have either one," she cried.

"Elly, I do have to ask you if you and Harry know Glenn Weaver."

Elly almost laughed at the question. "The art teacher? What does he have to do with this?"

"Possibly nothing, but there was a fire at his home last night, and he is also considered missing at this time."

"What is happening?" she sobbed. "Isabel and Harry and that other guy. What is happening?"

"So, you and Harry didn't know Glenn Weaver well?"

"He was just another teacher here. I don't know anything about him."

"Elly, I'm sorry I had to bring you the message about Harry. Please, let Ethan help you now. I'll return when we know anything of value."

Elly pulled herself together again. "I'm sorry, too, Don. Harry and I have much love and respect for you. I'm sorry you had to do this as well, but I trust you, and I know you'll take care of us."

SATURDAY NIGHT INTO SUNDAY

I t was close to midnight when the state coroner and investigation team wrapped up their work in the auditorium. Lieutenant Shane Mitchell had been hand-picked by Lester Timmons to take the state lead on the Churchville incidents. Don Weston and Rick Walker met Shane at the murder scene. They'd be working a lot together in the next few days.

From a distance, one might assume that Rick and Shane were twinning. They both stood roughly six feet tall with brown hair and wore the standard detective uniform of dark suit, white shirt, and understated tie. Similarities diverged from there. Rick was a forty-something mid-career Dad bod with brown eyes. Shane was ten years younger, sporting the chiseled body of a gym rat. His eyes were a striking blue.

"Chief Weston," said Shane. "I wish it were different circumstances, but I'm pleased to meet you in person. My boss, Lester Timmons, speaks very highly of you."

Don responded, "That's kind of him. We've had some shared ground over the years."

"I hope we'll find some downtime to talk. The colonel said I can learn a lot from you if I pay attention," said Shane. "My next stop is the fire scene. Maybe we can find time to get together tomorrow."

"Sorry, Shane," said Don with a smile. "It won't wait until tomorrow. This will be an all-nighter. Whenever you can break away from Glenn Weaver's place, you and I and Rick have some videos to watch. Rick and I saw the beginning of the president's assault, which brought us quickly to the auditorium. We may have the entire event captured, but this case is now in the State Police jurisdiction, and you're the lead investigator. I don't want to watch further until you can join us."

"I'll call when I'm on my way," said Shane. "That's definitely all-nighter material."

The Pennsylvania state investigation team moved to Glenn Weaver's property, which was already under the county sheriff's guard. In the interim period, auxiliary lighting had been set up at the barn scene so their work there would be under almost daylight conditions. The weather cooperated completely; it was calm and clear.

As promised, Chief Weston had asked the coroner to let Elly see the body before transport. The coroner had preliminarily estimated the time of death for Harold Olson between 9:00 p.m. and midnight last evening. Don Weston questioned himself for taking the Gettysburg trip. Had he been here, he thought, or if he had immediately returned when Elly contacted him, maybe things could have turned out differently.

More than twelve hours had passed between Harold Olson's death and the time of discovery. The intense heat of the stage lights greatly hastened the putrefaction process of the body, which would normally set in after about forty-eight hours. The coroner agreed to let Elly see her husband. Ethan McCallum was with her when Don came to get them. Don Weston warned Elly that it would be a very brief look and she couldn't touch Harry in any way.

"What happened to his beautiful hair?" was her first reaction, followed by more tears.

"We'll know much more soon," said Don as Ethan McCallum led the grieving widow back to her home.

At 2:00 a.m., the work started at Glenn Weaver's barn. A path and a clearing were opened to the body, and the contents from that cleaning would be sifted for other potential evidence. In a burning death, when a person is unconscious but still marginally alive, muscles contract, and the flexor muscles pull the limbs into a defensive position. Glenn had assumed that pugilistic stance in death. The coroner manipulated the body for further inspection and discovered a knife stuck in Glenn's chest. They would carefully transfer the human remains of Glenn Weaver as he was to join Harold Olson back in Harrisburg.

Preliminary searches of the house and outbuildings found an impressive crop of live cannabis, including the greenhouse and the Foamhenge garden, and an equally impressive storage of dried samples. Everything else in the house appeared normal and unremarkable. Fingerprints were taken from doors and the regular touch surfaces throughout. The suicide note was bagged and tagged. Arrangements were being made by the Pennsylvania State Police Department to have Mariposa police notify the next of kin. But who was James?

Shane Mitchell was able to leave the scene around 3:30 a.m. He called Chief Don Weston to let him know he was on his way for the video review.

THE SCENE ON STAGE

A little after 4:00 a.m., coffee was on, and the three investigators gathered in front of a smart board in a conference room by Don Weston's office. The chief picked up the interior auditorium cameras where he and Rick had first discovered the footage so Shane could see what they had seen. Harold Olson entered, walked to the lit stage, and gazed intently towards the ceiling. Now, Shane, too, watched as the shadow crept up behind the president, delivered a devastating kick to Olson's groin, and secured the victim's ankles and hands.

"Holy shit!' said Shane.

Don Weston stopped here with the suggestion that they should try to take in the whole scene. The auditorium cameras were not the highest resolution and had no zoom feature. They wouldn't be able to focus on small details, but they would be able to compare what they were seeing now with what they saw at the final crime scene. A hydraulic platform lift sat in the middle of the stage. A rope hung from above. The rope seemed to be attached to a stage light that was sitting on the floor. All the other stage lights appeared to be lit, throwing an intense illumination. Duly noted as the "before" picture. The movie continued. They all knew the "after" picture.

Don Weston took the camera off pause, beginning the riveting new footage for all three investigators. Harold Olson was secured by the assailant, who now tied him to the guardrail of the hydraulic platform. Something was wrapped around his head—something that the three men watching now knew to be a type of ball gag. The next twenty-five minutes of video involved the person in black securing the main doors of the auditorium. Don and Rick knew from conquering that obstacle what a thorough job that task was. It ended with the unknown assassin rolling a tool cart down the aisle and up the handicapped ramp to the stage.

The presumed murderer was greeted by the victim, well secured but thrashing wildly against the railing of the vertical lift. This was met with the introduction of a new tool from the cart: a longish rod of sorts. The tool was held to the victim's neck, a touch that immediately produced ten or so seconds of severe convulsions and then apparent unconsciousness.

"Stop," said Rick. "I think I know what that is. I even have one."

"Let's watch what else we have here first," said Shane. "You can fill us in later."

The shadow was using a sharp instrument to cut off Olson's hair and clothes, rendering him somewhat bald and naked. Several pulls of duct tape were then wrapped around Olson's head and the ball gag. The dark figure rolled the unconscious president around, side to side, and front to back, legs open, legs closed, as some sort of truss arrangement was made. The floor end of the rope was released from the stage light on the ground, revealing a noose, which was hung around the president's neck, and attached to the other hardware that had been assembled on his body. Olson stirred a couple of times through this process but was quickly convulsed and subdued by the application of the baton directly to his shaved scalp.

The inert Harold Olson was positioned on top of the hydraulic lift. That was the end of the viewable spectacle as the shadow closed the curtains. There were no cameras on the actual stage to see beyond the drapes. Don, Shane, and Rick sat silent for several minutes as it settled in that the show was over.

MOVIE REVIEWS

"**S**hane," Don said. "You're officially in charge of the investigation. What are your thoughts?"

"My first thought at the actual death scene earlier today was that President Olson was a sizable and toned human being. I thought that either there were multiple assailants or he had somehow submitted to part of the stage ritual before things went wrong. When the much smaller, dark figure appeared, I would have guessed, if I didn't already know the outcome, that Olson could have easily defended himself against any threat. In reality, by great, prior, creative planning, Olson never had a chance."

Shane turned to Rick now. "I short-stopped you when you said you knew what the stun weapon was. Can you fill us in? It was certainly a highly effective tool in subduing our victim."

"Well, I think it's the same thing," said Rick. "Last year, the Sheriff's Department had a booth at the Churchville town fair where we do our regular 'community service, get to know your police, register your dogs and children' thing. There was another booth near us that caught my attention with intermittent, crackling sounds, sharp and loud enough to make me jump the first few times I heard them. I struck up a conversation with the vendor there. She was a franchisee for a line of self-defense items for women.

"The array of products was fascinating, especially a prominently displayed stun baton for deterring a presumed giant-of-a-male attacker. My wife regularly walks her small Sheltie at night, and I bought her one of those. I guess everyone in law enforcement has been jolted by Tasers in training exercises, but I'd never dare to try this thing on myself. From the sound alone, I think I'd rather be shot than shocked by one of these things. I can't say for sure that's the tool our murderer had, but it certainly appears to be something similar."

Don laughed. "Not sure I'd rather be shot, but I do remember that event, and that booth, and I was curious about the products. Now that I know you have one of those things, we'll have to break it out and play with it sometime."

"Depending on how our investigation continues," said Lieutenant Mitchell. "We may be playing with that thing sooner than later. Switching gears, what do we think we know about our assailant from what we've seen on tape?"

"Not much," answered Detective Walker. "Average to smallish height and build, does seem to be quite strong for their size, any identifying marks, even gender, are masked by the clothing and the less-than-stellar video quality."

"Is there anything about the attacker that makes you think of any specific person from the school?" Shane asked Don Weston.

"Without any more detail, it could be anyone from at least fifty percent of the campus population," said Don.

"Well then," said Shane. "I need to be back in Harrisburg for tomorrow's—actually, today's—autopsies. I'll be in touch with any new results from that exercise, and I'll be back in person Monday. Any loose ends here?"

Don said this time, "I had a message from the local news outlet. Would you be comfortable if I take the lead on engaging with them? I have good relations with the reporter from past history. Something obviously will end up in the press. I'm hoping we can control some of the speculation and narrative until we know more."

"Chief Weston," said Lieutenant Mitchell. "I may be the official lead investigator on our pending case or cases, but you are far and away the most seasoned and experienced member of our cohort. I trust you implicitly to represent all of us on the news front."

"One more thing," said Don, chuckling. The others joined in the amusement when he added, "Why does that make me sound like Columbo? But seriously, I found a piece of what appears to be a tail-light lens near the driveway at our fire scene. It's probably nothing, but I bagged and tagged it just in case. I'm going to run it by our local car dealers' row Monday and see if it can be identified. No stone unturned."

Shane asked Rick if he had any other thoughts. Everyone was tired.

HARRISBURG

Dr. Maynard Ryan was the chief medical examiner and coroner for the Harrisburg office. He had pronounced the deaths of Harold Olson and Glenn Weaver at their respective scenes and arrived back in Harrisburg at 4:00 a.m. with their remains.

He'd seen worse in his career, but not much. These were possibly the two most gruesome bodies he'd had side by side on his examining tables in his thirty-five-year career. He would get a few hours of sleep before he began the autopsies, but he had one mission to complete before that. Harold Olson was being placed in a cold storage locker as Dr. Ryan started the process to retrieve the knife from Glenn Weaver's chest. He wanted this in the hands of the analyst and DNA technicians right now. It was unquestionably the most significant piece of hard evidence that was currently in play. Working on that piece of evidence 24/7 would likely still require a minimum sixty-hour turnaround. Dr. Ryan hoped to have that information back in the investigator's hands by Wednesday.

The two crime scenes, and the disappearance of Isabel Helms, were being considered by the state as potentially related events until proven otherwise. The DNA evidence from Isabel's house had just been finalized. It showed only one source. No clues to an assailant or intruder had surfaced, but the lab now had a DNA profile based on the samples from Isabel's house.

When the knife was retrieved and turned over to the lab, Glenn Weaver joined Harold Olson in cold storage, and Maynard Ryan went home to get some rest before autopsies began Sunday evening. Don Weston and Rick Walker had abdicated the case lead, but Colonel Lester Timmons, the head of the Pennsylvania State Police Bureau of Criminal Investigation, had reiterated to Shane Mitchell and his team that Don was a valuable, trusted resource and a friend. As such, Don would be informed on every step of the investigation, from the crime scene to forensics. Weston already had the news on Isabel's DNA. He'd also have the preliminary autopsy reports by Monday morning and the knife DNA results by Wednesday.

Alvin Corson from the York News Outlet WYCC had left a message on Don Weston's cell phone Saturday afternoon. He knew there had been a police presence on campus that day. Don and Alvin had an excellent working relationship from years of school publicity and reporting on Civil War reenactments locally. Don messaged back that it was just a training exercise and nothing newsworthy, but that he'd call him again soon. Now, on Sunday morning, he messaged Alvin Corson for a lunch date.

LUNCH AT
CASA POLERA

Alvin Corson and Don Weston met at a local Mexican restaurant they had frequented many times before. They had become friends over the past several years, both professionally and socially, and enjoyed each other's company. Alvin sensed very early that this was a professional meeting.

Alvin Corson had been with WYCC for over twenty-five years and now served as their daily news anchor. He was a small, mousy-haired presence in person but a big deal locally. WYCC was the largest and most influential news source in the immediate area, broadcasting from the city of York, Pennsylvania. Alvin could be found doing county fairs, farm reports, football games, and grand openings. He also happened to be a competent investigative journalist and very trusted with the serious news of the day.

"What's up, Don?"

"Let's order and I'll fill you in on my past week."

Chips, salsa, and iced tea arrived, and the orders were placed. Don spoke quietly, "I trust you, Alvin, and some of what I share may have to remain confidential."

"I trust you, too, Don, and I understand, as always."

"This all started last Monday, and we've had several incidents surrounding university personnel that may or may not be related."

"Such as?"

"On Monday morning, the university provost, Isabel Helms, did not show up for work and hasn't been seen since. The police traffic you noted yesterday was not a training exercise. University President

Harold Olson was reported missing Friday evening. We discovered his body in the auditorium yesterday afternoon."

"Don, you know I have to report that; what were the circumstances?"

"I'll leave it for now as expected foul play. There's more."

"More? I'm ready."

"An art teacher, Glenn Weaver, also went missing."

"I know Glenn; I've covered many of his showings. What's going on with him?"

"There was a fire at his home up on the hill."

"I knew there was a fire on the mountain yesterday afternoon; we thought it was just a brush fire and didn't even follow up on it."

"It was at his home. The barn was destroyed."

"And Glenn?"

"A body was recovered at the scene. It's believed to be Glenn; we're awaiting identification from the coroner's office. There was a possible suicide note at the scene. That's everything."

Food had arrived, and both men started eating. It was another minute or two before anyone said anything. It was Alvin who spoke first, "Don, what do you want me to do?"

"I know you need to report on Harold Olson's death, but I'd like it left for now as mysterious circumstances, pending investigation. I wanted you to know the total circumstances of the three disappearances. The discovery of a body in a fire at Glenn Weaver's home is also a news event. Without positive, legal identification of Glenn, that would be a presumably unrelated incident at this time but certainly coincidental that both were employed at Churchville University. I'd prefer that you don't disclose the possible suicide note at this time. I'd also prefer the missing-person report of Isabel Helms be downplayed as pure coincidence at this point. It's possible that someone misinterpreted vacation dates, and she may even show up at her office tomorrow morning. There is no evidence to support anything else surrounding her absence."

"Well, I must open tonight with the Olson death. I'll be at the auditorium this afternoon with a film crew to cover that. I'll also check with the local fire officials on details from the barn burning. I'll hold onto the missing provost story until tomorrow if you think it could be simple confusion on vacation dates, but let me know if she doesn't show up then. You know the Olson story will be picked up in a larger arena, and other reporters could begin to appear in the next day from at least Philadelphia and Harrisburg."

"I know that; there's nothing we can do to stop it."

"How soon can you give me more information?"

"I should have a positive ID on the body from the barn fire by tomorrow morning. If it is Glenn, then I'll give you a partial picture of the letter he left. I'll also let you know if Isabel Helms shows up tomorrow. We're still days away from positive forensic examination on anything else, but I'll give you as full a disclosure as possible as events change."

"That's fair. I'll be at the auditorium at 3:00 to interview you for the Olson story."

"That's fair, too. Let's finish lunch. With all that is going on, I never know when I'll eat or sleep again."

AUTOPSY

Lieutenant Shane Mitchell was the lead crime scene investigator at the auditorium and barn. Per department protocol, he joined Maynard Ryan at the autopsy tables at 3:00 p.m. Sunday. Another evidence technician had already removed the paper bags from the hands of the corpses and the zip ties from Olson. He'd also picked stray dirt and debris from the clothing and bodies and started the scraping of fingernails.

"Welcome again, Shane," said the Doctor.

"Always a pleasure," said the lieutenant.

"Get any sleep?"

"Very little. You?"

"Enough, I guess. I see you already got the knife passed on to the lab."

"Did it as soon as we got here. It was an out-the-front switchblade. A great candidate for DNA even with the burn factor."

"Well," Shane said. "That could be our only good news so far. I stopped by the lab on the way up. Fluid tests confirmed what we thought we knew from the scene at the school. Everything on the machine platform and the floor puddles match Olson; the rest was hydraulic leakage from the scissors' jack. Nothing there to link a perpetrator."

"Hopefully, we'll turn up something here to give you a suspect," said the doctor. "Let's do the president first. He should be the interesting one. I'll be surprised if our burn/stab guy presents more than the obvious. Final exam, Mr. President."

Examination of the head and neck was the first step since there was no clothing to remove. A technician had already weighed and measured both bodies. The neck was not broken by the hanging. Every step was recorded by audio as the coroner proceeded. Every injury or anomaly was photographed and also noted on a body chart, no matter how small or seemingly insignificant. The petechial rash was noted in the eyes, as expected in strangulation.

Dr. Ryan removed the duct tape and ball gag. The scalp was carefully examined, producing findings of multiple, small cuts, apparently from the head shaving. There were also several spots with double, reddish, dot-like lesions. These were consistent with the application of some type of stun gun. Another of these same wounds was noted on the neck. Shane already knew that was how Olson was subdued.

When the external head and neck observations were completed, Dr. Ryan cut the scalp from ear to ear, folded the skin up over the face and down over the neck, and proceeded to open the skull with a cranial saw. The brain was extracted and found to be normal in all appearances. Moving to the chest, a Y-shaped incision was made, the skin was retracted, and the ribcage was split with rib shears. Organs were individually examined, and samples and fluids were taken, but no abnormalities were found. Donald Olson had been a well-muscled, lean, and healthy specimen of a man just forty-eight hours ago.

The genital area was grossly disfigured. A razor-wire strand had been pulled through this area, starting at the base of the scrotum. The body was effectively emasculated, with the genital remains, hanging from minimal skin, stuck to a bow tie by dried blood. The assessment of this wound, the bleeding patterns from the scene, and the condition of the lungs concluded this injury was completed after death. The official cause of death was asphyxiation by hanging.

Maynard Ryan and Shane Mitchell completed their notes. There were no defensive wounds found on the body of Harold Olson. A medical assistant moved to complete tissue sampling and ultimate closure of the Olson corpse. Maynard and Shane washed up and changed to turn their attention to Glenn Weaver. They started again with the head and neck area. The doctor's assistant had already carefully removed articles of clothing, essentially the remains of a t-shirt, leather coveralls, socks, and boots.

"Between the knife wound and the burns, there's no need to examine the brain in this one," said Ryan.

Head and neck showed no trauma beyond the fire damage, no broken bones, and no other wounds. They moved directly to the torso and made the same Y incision. The charred skin was reluctantly retracted, and Dr. Ryan was beginning to remove and examine organs when he stopped. "I've changed my mind on the cranial dissection." He was looking at a collection of telltale, grayish-white dots and small, firm lesions with wiry tentacles. "This man is riddled with cancer."

The organs were removed, sampled, and placed in formalin for the possible event of further examination. The skull-opening procedure was completed as it had been on Harold Olson, and the brain was removed. Further initial dissection revealed metastasis here as well. On the underside, one tentacled tumor, readily visible, engaged the amygdala.

The knife wound had only nicked the heart superficially. The burns he suffered as he was dying would have been fatal on their own. Based on the lung examination, Glenn Weaver's official cause of death would be asphyxiation caused by inhaling the byproducts of the fire.

"But," said Maynard Ryan. "This man would have been dead soon anyway from widespread, metastasized cancer."

The pathology fluids and organ samples were collected. Maynard washed and changed again to visit the evidence lab while the medical assistant began the process of closing and storing the second body.

SUNDAY EVENING NEWS

As the autopsy was underway in Harrisburg, Alvin Corson and Don Weston met again outside the Churchville auditorium. The imposing edifice secured with crime-scene tape would be the backdrop for the WYCC interview, the broadcast to be aired at 6:00 p.m.

Don had visited Elly Olson after lunch to let her know there would be a news story tonight. He warned her that, after that break, she would likely be a target for follow-up interviews. Ethan McCallum had spent the night in a guest room at the president's house and used Don's visit to do a quick run back to his place for a shower and to pack a bag. He would stay with her until she had other support. Don let Elly know she was not required to take any interview requests. He promised that, if she chose to engage with the media, he or Ethan would be available and by her side. She had called the children earlier, and both were on their way to be with her.

WYCC cameras and sound equipment were already in place and tested when Don Weston joined Corson at 3:00 p.m. Corson did an intro piece on the background of the school and its importance to the community, warning the audience that the recent events here were grim. He introduced Don Weston as the police chief and started the questions.

"Don, can you tell us what happened here in this auditorium?"

"At 10:00 a.m. yesterday, myself and Detective Rick Walker from the County Sheriff's Department came to this site to follow up on a missing person report. The missing person was Dr. Harold Olson, president of Churchville University. We found that access to the building had been blocked from the inside, and we enlisted local

Fire Department assistance. At approximately noon, we made entry to the building and discovered the body of Dr. Olson."

"Can you tell us what led you to this location?"

"Campus security cameras were reviewed yesterday morning. Dr. Olson was sighted around 3:00 p.m., leaving his office and making his way here. There was no record of him departing from here."

"Can you describe the circumstances of his death?"

"Alvin, no, I can't disclose any more at this time. The investigation is now in the hands of the Pennsylvania State Police. Evidence recovered here is already under review, a process that began last evening. I will state that Dr. Olson was a victim of foul play, but the exact nature and cause of death are still under investigation. I'm continuing as a resource to the state and will be informed as new information becomes available. I promise to let you know as results from the evidence and ongoing investigation are confirmed."

"Our viewers will appreciate that, Don. This is a very disturbing event for our local communities, and we owe the residents all the story. Have you identified a suspect, and is there any reason to believe there is an ongoing risk for the community?"

"We have a person of interest, but they are not currently a suspect, and I can't disclose the name at this time. There is no concern for community risk related to this event. We have one single murder scene that appears to be personal."

"Don, you told me earlier that there is another case of a missing employee from Churchville University. Can you expand on that for our viewers?"

"Only to say that one of our faculty members' homes was the scene of a fire yesterday. A body was recovered at the scene. The remains are pending formal identification and next-of-kin notification before we release any further statements."

"Do you think the disappearances are related?"

"Alvin, that would be speculation at this point, but we haven't ruled anything out. We understand two missing employees is an unusual coincidence. Are we done here? I am expecting some calls from the State Police on autopsy results."

"Don, thank you for your time. I know this is especially difficult as you have a personal relationship with President Olson and his family. Please let us know when you can share more information on these two cases."

That interview aired on Sunday at 6:00 p.m. A follow-up story confirmed that the Saturday fire was at the residence of Glenn Weaver, a visiting art professor at the university.

LAB UPDATE

Back in Harrisburg, Lieutenant Shane Mitchell and Dr. Maynard Ryan delivered the pathology samples from the two bodies to the crime lab. They met in the conference room with Dr. Earl Frost and several forensic technicians. Dr. Frost was the director of the lab. He held an MS degree in Forensic Science and a PhD in Forensic Chemistry. He also had almost thirty years of experience in the field. Frost was an exceptionally skilled asset for Pennsylvania State's main criminal lab.

The lead criminal investigator, the coroner, and the lab director, with input from the lab techs, reviewed what they thought they knew, what they didn't know, and what evidence was still in play. The three persons of interest, Isabel Helms, Harold Olson, and Glenn Weaver, were related concerns. Isabel Helms was still a missing person first reported six days ago. In the interim period, the lab had established a DNA profile for her. From the investigation of her residence and office, there was no evidence of abduction or foul play. She was simply missing. Harold Olson was dead. The cause of death was asphyxiation by hanging. A post-mortem severance of his scrotum and attached penis would also have caused a fatal injury, but he was confirmed to have already been deceased when that event occurred. Video review had shown that a stun gun of unknown origin had been applied repeatedly to his head and neck to keep him incapacitated while he was stripped and trussed. They had no weapon.

Glenn Weaver was dead. The cause of death was also asphyxiation from the elements of the fire. Whether it was simple asphyxiation or chemical asphyxiation could be determined by further examination of the lungs. It didn't matter for the criminal investigation. Glenn's suicide note and the evidence present at his property implied a clear, self-inflicted death but did not completely rule out a possible assailant.

His cancer was profoundly metastasized throughout his organs. No single organ was debilitated to the point that he would have been physically incapacitated at the time of death. His remaining life, however, would have been brief, and he would have been disabled very soon. The knife wound to Glenn's chest was deemed superficial and non-life-threatening. The condition of the body confirmed the asphyxiation definition, and there was no significant blood loss. The knife was currently disassembled in the lab, and the residue from the weapon was already in the starting processes of blood typing and DNA analysis.

Dr. Frost was focused on the cancer metastasis to the brain. "How familiar are you gentlemen with Charles Whitman?"

Shane Mitchell answered first, "Wasn't he the Texas tower shooter?"

"Yes," said Frost. "In 1966, Charles Whitman, possibly the first mass shooter in memory for most of us, fired indiscriminately from a tower at the University of Texas in Austin. He was also shot and killed that day. The ultimate death total for his work stood at sixteen adults and one unborn child." Shane inquired how that pertained to today's discussion. Dr. Maynard Ryan already had more than a clue. Frost continued, "When I was doing my graduate work in forensic science, I had an adjunct instructor, Fletcher Dixon, who had worked with Coleman de Chenar. De Chenar was the neuropathologist from Austin State Hospital who performed the autopsy on Charles Whitman."

"And?" Shane said again.

"A brain tumor was found pressing on the amygdala, much like the condition of Mr. Weaver. The medical research literature has since produced some seventeen other examples where seemingly normal persons who suddenly engaged in abnormal behavior produced autopsy results bearing this same condition. Of course, correlation does not equal evidence of causation, and there is no definitive test to link the anomaly. The Whitman story has always fascinated me, and this is the first time in my career that I've seen this potential connection."

"So," Shane said. "You're telling me that Glenn might have been influenced by this tumor to kill Olson?"

Dr. Ryan said this time, "He is telling us that you might consider it as part of your profiling in the investigation. These types of tumors have been noted in cases where upstanding, law-abiding citizens have suddenly committed horrific acts totally out of character. Evidentially there is no current scientific method to establish proof of cause to that."

"Okay," said the lieutenant. "We know for sure that Isabel is missing. We have a DNA profile from articles found at her residence. Without her physical presence, we can't definitively say that DNA is hers. We're proceeding with that assumption for now, but it would be challenged in a court of law. We also know the causes of death for our two corpses, and we have what we need to establish their DNA profiles."

"We don't have the stun gun weapon used on Dr. Olson. We have a suicide note for Glenn, and we don't know who 'James' is or if it matters. We have some suspicion that Glenn was not at his best due to his medical condition. We can't say for sure if there was only one assailant at either scene, but we have no evidence that supports any other conclusion."

"We're still likely three days from the DNA evidence on the knife. Do we know any more about that weapon?"

A forensic technician piped up, "We've identified the weapon as a Mago brand name, eleven-inch White Marble Italian Stiletto OTF Auto Knife with a five-inch blade. This is a dual-action knife, meaning the trigger both ejects and retracts the blade. The knife was disassembled this morning, and multiple blood samples were found between the blade and the internal mechanism. Two of the blood types match the cadavers in the morgue. Further testing will no doubt verify a positive match to the victims. The third type is a rare, AB-positive sample. It would be interesting to find the missing Isabel Helms has an AB-positive blood type, but that's not something we can determine from the hair DNA samples taken from her home.

"Wow, wow, wow!" said Shane. "You guys are amazing. Keep up the good work and get us DNA ASAP. I guess the ball is in my court for some more fieldwork now. I'll circle back to Don Weston and the county detective to share what we know. They did all the work of the first six days and they're physically in Churchville. They're excellent resources for us. I'll ask them if they can verify the blood type for Isabel Helms, find Glenn's oncologist, and who the hell James is. From here, we can continue evidence mining, including Glenn's home computer, while we wait on the DNA profiles."

BACK IN CHURCHVILLE

Sunday evening, Don got the call and review from Shane Mitchell. He called York County Sheriff Bill Hester to let him know he needed Detective Rick Walker back to help him with the assignments from the State Police Office. Bill assured him that Rick would be at Don's office at 8:00 a.m. Monday.

Rick was right on time for coffee and the morning review. Both Rick and Don were personally invested in this situation and were glad to keep an ongoing, official role. No surprise that the charred body was Glenn, but it was a big surprise that three blood types were on the knife and one of them didn't match the two victims. The biggest surprise would be if it did match, at least preliminarily, with Isabel Helms.

They felt marginally better that Harold Olson was dead and gone before his private parts were unceremoniously severed. Don still secretly wondered if all of it could have been avoided if he'd stayed home for the weekend. That was a private question that would never have an answer.

Per Don, Rick would take the role of lead investigator in their current and future work together on the case. The state and county police departments worked very closely, formally and informally. Don Weston had connections across both, and his department was the epicenter of the investigation, but Rick had an official government role and linkage that Don did not. To keep things above reproach, they would use the formal reporting mechanism of the county to work with the state. Don had covered this adjustment during his call with Shane Mitchell, and Shane agreed it was an appropriate move.

The day started with several courtesy calls, one by phone and two in person. As promised, Don touched base with Alvin Corson at WYCC. After pleasantries were exchanged, Don shared, "Alvin, the burned body from Glenn's residence is indeed Glenn. I know you'll have to report that. I don't have anything else to report on either of the deaths currently. I also reviewed security cameras on campus just now. They don't show any Isabel Helms sightings this morning."

"Thanks, Don. How would you like me to handle the missing provost at this point?"

"Hold it until the evening update. Make it clear that it is not known to be related to other campus events, but if the public has any knowledge of her whereabouts over the past week, they should get in touch with appropriate authorities."

"Got it; keep me posted."

"I promised I would."

"Don, one more thing that might help on your end. I'm going to call the closest metro areas, Philadelphia and Harrisburg, to share our interview and the news on Glenn. I have very good friends and sources at the key stations. I'll do everything I can to keep them physically at bay if possible. That will probably only work for a few days, but it might make things easier for you and the investigators."

"Alvin, that would be a great service if you can pull it off. In a few days, we expect to have the DNA evidence that would put together many loose ends. I appreciate your offer. Good luck with that."

They next stopped at Isabel Helms' house. The neighbors or the school had mowed the lawn so all looked normal. Don's seal was still intact on the front door when he opened it with Elly's key. This would be a quick trip. They still didn't have a warrant or cause to break into the wardrobe in the garage, but they likely would very soon.

They went straight to the medicine cabinet. Isabel had an unusually spartan medicine cabinet with just a couple of personal items. Isabel apparently had no physical conditions requiring medication. The only pills present were Tylenol, some vitamins, and a compact-sized disc of birth control pills. Fortunately, the pharmacy label listing the prescribing physician's name was with the pills.

Isabel did her business with the Churchville CVS on the outskirts of town. Likely everyone in Churchville did the same. The prescribing physician was Dr. Regina Woods. By coincidence, Dr. Woods was also Don's general practitioner. Her office came next.

Rick and Don presented their badges when they entered the physician's office. They explained to the receptionist, a young woman who recognized Don, that this was an official visit and they needed to see Dr. Woods. The receptionist went to get her.

"Hey Chief, to what do I owe the honor today?" she said cheerily as she entered the waiting area.

"Dr. Woods, this is Detective Rick Walker with the County Sheriff's Office, can we visit with you in your office for a few minutes? This is an official police matter that needs some privacy." Don said all that feeling overly formal and imposing.

"Come on back to my office," said Dr. Woods.

Rick was officially in charge but let Don do the talking since he knew the doctor. "Dr. Woods."

"Come on, Don, it's me, Regina."

"Of course, sorry, Regina. It's been a long week in police mode."

"I get it. I heard about the college president and the other thing with the fire. You certainly do have a handful."

"We need your help with some information on a patient."

"You know that depends on the HIPAA rules if I can help or not."

"We are well aware of that and wouldn't ask you to compromise in any way. This one you can help with. It's an official missing person case, and we have some reason to believe it may be related to two deaths."

"Wow, Don, I can certainly disclose anything you need based on that."

"I need you to keep our conversation confidential. You will have some information that has not been publicly reported, and I need you to keep it that way for now. You do understand?"

"Certainly. Not a concern."

"A patient of yours, Miss Isabel Helms, was reported missing one week ago. There has been no sign of her whereabouts since that time. We found some pills at her home with a pharmacy label listing you as the prescribing physician."

"That would be birth control pills, her only prescription. She's a very healthy woman. Oh no, now you've got me worried, I love that perky Miss Isabel."

"Is there anything in her medical history that would be a concern to you as her primary care physician?"

"Absolutely nothing."

"We have a DNA profile from some articles found in her home. Can you confirm her blood type for us?"

"I can do that," she said, swiveling to the computer on the credenza behind her. It only took a minute. "Type AB-positive," she said. "That's a rare one."

"Thank you, that's all we need to know for now. If there's more, we'll get back to you."

"Still nice seeing you, Don. I hope Isabel turns up okay."

"So do I," Don said, now certain that Isabel was also dead.

On the way back to the Churchville campus, Detective Rick Walker connected with Lieutenant Shane Mitchell by phone. Based on the rarity of the blood type, they all considered this another death investigation.

The next courtesy call was a trip across campus to Elly Olson. Elly looked very tired when she answered the door. Don was glad to see that the children were with her now.

"Have you found anything more on Harry and Isabel?" she asked.

He was respectfully direct in his answer. "No change on Isabel's disappearance, but I can tell you that the body at Glenn Weaver's place was Glenn. That appears to be a suicide. The cause of death for Glenn was directly related to the fire, but that has not been reported, so I ask you to keep that confidential. I can also tell you that Harry's cause of death was asphyxiation. I still can't disclose details, but I wanted you to know he was unconscious and not in pain when he passed away." Probably at least a partial mistruth.

"Why can't I know what happened to him? Did that Glenn guy kill him?" Her voice was raising now.

"Elly, I promise to keep you informed. Rick and I are following up on several leads today, and we hope to be able to share all the answers very soon." Harold Jr. and Cindy Olson, now young adults, drew closer to their mother, and Harold had his hand on her shoulder as he spoke.

"Mom, Chief Weston is doing everything that can be done right now. Let's let him do his job, and we'll know everything about Dad soon."

Don gave young Harold a nod of sincere thanks as he and Rick departed.

NEXT CHORES

Another task for the day was to talk with Glenn's oncology doctor. They hoped to find out who that was through the school clinic, which was the first point of call for sick students and faculty.

The school nurse knew Chief Weston and greeted him warmly. Don again took the lead and felt overly formal. The script was the same. "This is Detective Rick Walker with the County Sheriff's Office; can we visit with you in your office for a few minutes? This is an official police matter that needs some privacy."

"Anything for you, Don; is this about the president?"

"Not directly. I'm looking for some information regarding Glenn Weaver."

"I heard he was missing."

"Unfortunately, he is now known to be dead."

She sat down and put her face in her hands and began to cry. "This is so sad," she sobbed. "They are both such nice men. What is happening?" That seemed to be the universal response across campus.

Don said, "We're working on the criminal investigations of both deaths. I'm sure you know that HIPAA allows the release of information under these circumstances. I need to know if you can help me find Glenn's oncologist. The autopsy revealed an advanced cancer, and his doctor may be able to assist with some information in the organ analysis."

"I knew Glenn had some health issues, but I didn't realize it was that bad. He came to me at the beginning of the semester with an annoying cough. Let's call Brian Rowe. He's the physician we use for school referrals and the first doctor that Glenn would have seen."

She made the call. Dr. Rowe had found results, potentially indicative of cancer, from lung X-rays. He then referred Glenn to an oncology resident at UPMC Medical Center. The doctor was contacted and said he could be available to meet with the two investigators in the next hour.

"Thank you," Don said to the school nurse. "This is difficult for everyone in the Churchville family, and you've been extremely helpful."

They let the oncology resident know that Glenn Weaver was dead, and he confirmed what they already knew from the autopsy. The history was the review of the lung X-ray, biopsy, and an initial CUP diagnosis, or carcinoma of unknown primary. A full-body CT/PET scan revealed widespread metastasis. Further testing identified the likely primary cancer as pancreatic.

Detective Rick Walker asked, "Doctor, can you give us a minute to call the state medical examiner?"

"Certainly; let me know if there's anything else I can do. Mr. Weaver seemed like a very nice guy. Unfortunately, his disease was well-involved when we met him. We would have nothing to offer but palliative and hospice care as it progressed."

Dr. Maynard Ryan requested a copy of the last CT/PET scan to compare with findings at death. The oncologist spoke with Ryan and made that happen while Don and Rick were still there. The two men had a very productive day thus far, and it was still early. It was time to grab a quick bite. Don and Rick pondered the next steps over another Casa Polera visit.

Even without a DNA match, the unique blood type finding and the circumstances would be enough to secure a warrant to do a more exhaustive search, including the locked wardrobe at Isabel's house. AB-positive blood was not quite as rare as AB-negative, but it was rare enough at less than 4% share of the White population. That would likely be the Tuesday agenda. They were hoping to get some traction on "James" first.

Glenn Weaver didn't appear to have any real social circle. They concluded that if they wanted to find anyone close to Glenn, they would have to start with Glenn himself, beginning from the at-the-end clue. Don suggested, and Rick agreed, that a quick round of contacts with other art faculty and a review of current student names would be next.

Back on campus, Don pulled up the class rosters of Glenn's current students. Surprisingly, only one James made the list. The rosters had cell phone numbers for the students, and they called him. It turned out he was a business professor who had signed up for the metal art class just for a break in routine. He never actually got to attend any of the classes, thanks to the general upheaval and increased demands on faculty during this semester. He thought Glenn was a fun guy. He liked him but didn't know him well. He never mentioned if he'd seen the news on the fire, and they never mentioned the current state of Glenn.

Don and Rick headed to walk the rounds of the Art Department offices and labs. Everyone was gone on Spring Break except the department chair, Franklin Santos. Again, Don delivered the usual, "Frank, this is Detective Rick Walker with the County Sheriff's Office. This is an official police matter."

Franklin was stunned at the confirmation of Glenn's death. Glenn didn't seem to have any close friends, but he and Franklin had been as close as anyone that Glenn might have known. They did a lot of art together, coordinated classes, and shared a few beers after work, maybe even the occasional joint. Franklin might have been the only person to spend time with Glenn at his home studio and was able to provide details on the pre-fire barn and its contents.

"Glenn liked old-school clay throwing. He had four different kilns in the shop. One was a rare, wood-fired, Japanese antique. Glenn told me his dad had one of these and Glenn loved the different glazing it produced. I think he also loved that it connected him to his dad; they were very close. He had two other antiques: classic American kilns, one also wood-fired and one coal-fired. The fourth kiln was a modern, gas-fired oven. It produced much higher temperatures that were controllable in a sustainable way. The old kilns were great for the real, artsy results, not always predictable, but, as clay artists, we love that the kiln is a creative participant in the result. The gas oven could make consistent, reproducible ceramics for, say, sets of plates.

"He also had complete wood and art shops in separate areas of the barn. Glenn was a very creative and talented guy. His pottery was unique and varied, and his woodwork was as good as any cabinet maker. He liked metal sculpture and could crank it out in any appropriate method. There's a lot of his work all over the campus."

Rick stated, "You certainly seem to know Glenn as well as anyone we've talked to, and you're the only person we've encountered who visited his home and shop. Can you tell us about anyone else in the department, on campus, or in the local community who may have been as close to him?"

"Not that I know of. I never met anyone that didn't like Glenn, but I never met anyone that clicked with him either. Glenn is a unique character. I might compare him to an old Robin Williams monologue: his mind spewed creativity, and it could change direction at any second. I loved that, but most non-art folks seemed to find it difficult to maintain a coherent conversation." Franklin laughed at that statement. "Really a unique character.

"When he was on campus, he was either in class or in the studio. He didn't participate in the politics of faculty meetings and committees. He just stayed in his craft. We had lunch at the student cafeteria regularly. Students loved him. He just didn't care for the academic side that spoke in ontologies and pedagogies. Many of us were jealous of his freedom from the status quo, but that position also made him more vulnerable to not having his contract renewed. He was out of sight, and out of mind, to the administration. Just that odd guy that wanders."

Don said, "Frank, do you know of anyone in Glenn's life by the name of James? We're trying to follow up on some correspondence from Glenn's home that seems to indicate he was recently close to a James."

"I can't think of a James off the top of my head, and I don't recall him mentioning anyone by that name recently. The only other person I know who he had some friendship with would be Erin Eland at York County Community College. The campus has a nice art facility with a public gallery. Glenn often had his work on display there and visited the shows of other artists in rotation at the school."

"Thanks for your time, Frank," Don said. "I have some contacts at YCCC in campus security. I'll reach out to them for anything on Glenn's shows and try to visit with Erin Eland. I'd like to ask one favor of you. Could you make calls to the other art faculty and see if James rings a bell for anyone else? I know they're all off campus for break, but I'd appreciate it if you could touch base with them as a favor to me. I don't expect they know any more than you do, but it will save me some time so Rick and I can follow up on YCCC right away."

"Absolutely. I can call you back in probably the next hour to let you know if there's anything there. Do you think that Glenn and Harold Olson are related in any way? This all seems too coincidental and weird."

"I can't say we have anything confirmed yet one way or the other. But, yes, it all seems coincidental and weird to us as well. Send me a message on your phone calls with your faculty."

YORK COUNTY COMMUNITY COLLEGE

On the way to the YCCC campus, Don called their head of security, Tony Hoffman. Don had been the consultant on their latest upgrades in their security monitoring, so they knew each other well. YCCC had a similar camera network to the Churchville campus, and Don hoped it could help. During the call, Tony was able to confirm that Erin Eland was on campus that day.

Rick and Tony already knew each other as well; they first met a couple of years back. Tony had asked the county for help with some tagging incidents on campus. They eventually detained some high school students. The parents of the involved youths were not any happier than the college about the incident. All parties agreed that corrective action would be a complete and total cleaning of impacted campus walls and signage, the labor provided by the perpetrators. Case closed. Since then, Rick had joined the adjunct faculty staff.

Tony put Erin Eland on speakerphone in his office. "Erin, it's Tony Hoffman with campus security. Do you have a minute to talk with police investigators about Glenn Weaver?"

"Yes. I heard about the fire at his place on Saturday. I don't know what I can do to help, but I'm open for the next hour. Do you need me there at your office?"

"No, we have some quick review to do here, but they'd probably like a tour of the art center. I'll bring them to you shortly."

"Thank you, Tony."

"One more thought; do you know when the last Glenn Weaver show was on campus?"

"Certainly; it was a metal sculpture showing and sale. It was just a couple of weeks ago."

"Excellent, see you soon."

Don said, "Okay, Tony, let's hit the cameras."

"Don, I hate to disappoint you on this one. We converted from the thirty-day save to a seven-day loop about six months ago. I have nothing more than a week back."

"That is a disappointment. I'm sure you thought you had good reason to change from the protocol we set up. This case might give pause to re-address it, but that's a philosophical point for later. I guess all we can do now is visit with Erin Eland."

On the walk across campus, Don got his message from Franklin Santos. No James recollection from the other art faculty. Erin Eland was their last open thread. Tony made the introduction this time. "Erin, this is Don Weston, Chief of Police at Churchville University, and Detective Rick Walker with the County Sheriff's Office. This is an official police matter."

"How can I help?" she asked.

Erin was a tall, slender, smiling woman in her sixties. Her outfit was a brightly colored and patterned sundress and sandals. She had long, straight gray hair and no makeup. Don thought she could have been Joni Mitchell with her artsy, creative, hippy-ish vibe.

"Erin," Don started. "How well did you know Glenn Weaver?"

Erin's smile faded. "That's a past-tense question."

Don, direct as always, said, "We were able to confirm last night that the body at the Weaver property was indeed Glenn. I'm sorry."

Tears welled up in Erin's eyes now. "What a tragic loss. He was such a nice guy and a truly gifted artist. What happened?"

"I can tell you there was a fire of unknown origin at his barn, and that's where he was found. I don't have any other information to share currently. The cause and circumstances are still under investigation."

"How about the university president who died? Were they together?"

"Different crime scenes, different circumstances, and no current connection by evidence, but we are looking for any leads on both deaths. Can you show us the gallery where Glenn's last show was held?"

"It's right down the hall from here; let's go." As they followed through the building, she remarked, "Some of Glenn's pieces are still on display on the walls. He made these fascinating facemasks, mostly from farm equipment scrap, like machine blades and old tools."

As they entered the gallery, Don saw the faces right away. He had seen some of them before at a Churchville campus display. The collection would probably be labeled "whimsical," but they ranged from funny to creepy to downright scary. Creative and well-made, Glenn's work did draw one in.

"Erin, how close were you with Glenn Weaver?"

"I'd say we were art friends. His work is displayed here regularly with a quarterly show schedule of rotating local artists. Glenn Weaver's pottery and sculptures are quite collectible. He's probably the most well-known and critically acclaimed artist we work with. I don't know that he has many personal relationships. He's very fun and pleasant, but there's also an artistic aloofness. He seemed especially distant and preoccupied on his last visit. I still would have been attracted to him if we were both young and carefree."

"We found a reference in his writings that indicated a thank you to a James, apparently for being recently supportive of him. Would you have any idea who James might be?"

"Well, James Giles was here all three nights of Glenn's last showing. I'm sure you know him. He's the former dean at Churchville. He used to come to the faculty art shows from there, but I hadn't seen him in a couple of years. I was surprised to see James turn up at this show."

"Do you know James Giles well?"

Erin smiled at the question. "I don't know if Dr. Giles wants anyone to know him well. He's not a warm, inviting people person. He's a short, slight man, naturally effeminate in his mannerisms. His appearance projects polite and modest, but his words and actions project command and control. Every time I've met him, he made it clear that he was to be respected as a very important person. I think the ego is compensation for a real inferiority complex.

"That's the only James I can think of for Glenn. I've never met Glenn's parents, but I know he was very close with them. He talked about his visits with them all the time. I believe their names were Sally and Michael, so no James there."

"Thank you, Irene; you've been very helpful."

"Please let me know if there's anything else I can do. This is all so sad."

"That was an interesting revelation," said Don to Rick as they got to the car.

"I take it you know James Giles."

"Quite well. I'm not sure how or if it fits in our puzzle, but it is interesting."

AUTO ROW

It was 3:30 when the three men left. Don and Rick parted ways with Tony in the parking lot and headed back into town. They still had time to shop Don's taillight lens around Auto Row. They stopped at the Toyota dealer first. Don knew the dealer principal there and dropped by his office to say hi. Daniel Sorkum owned several dealerships in the surrounding metro areas. He had just opened this store two years ago. Don knew him from his Philadelphia days.

"Hi, Daniel, what's new in your business?" said Don.

"Don!" he responded warmly. "We're good. It seems all the real news is in your business lately."

"You hit that nail on the head."

"What's going on at the school? I knew Harold Olson well, and he was a great guy. How could anyone not like him, let alone want to kill him?"

"You and the rest of the world will know that as soon as I do, I promise."

"So, what brings you here? I'd be happy to put you in a new Sequoia as a patrol vehicle or maybe an Avalon or Camry for your personal ride," said the perpetual salesman.

"Thanks, Dan, but I think the vehicles you already sold me will probably never wear out, so I'm good on the transportation front. What I'm looking for today is this," he said, holding out the evidence bag with the broken lens inside.

"Is that part of the investigation?"

"Possibly not, just a fishing trip at this point. I'm going to show it to your parts guys and see if they can identify it."

"They're the best in the business," said Dan proudly. "If anyone can help, it will be those guys. I'll call and tell them you're on your way. Anything else I can do to help?"

"Nothing I can think of. I have a couple more tasks to wrap up today, and we'll fill the local news in if we make any breaks in our search. Take care," Chief Weston said as he and Rick made their way to the parts department.

No luck at Toyota, so they continued down the row of dealers. No luck at Chevrolet or Ford. No luck at Honda or Kia. They were running low on options when Chief Weston approached the parts counter at the Subaru store. A young guy wearing the dealership's casual, golf shirt uniform greeted him with, "How can I help you?"

Don displayed the evidence bag for the sixth time and was astounded to hear, "Mid-model Subaru Outlander, right rear tail-light. I may still have one in stock."

"You're good!" said an impressed Don Weston.

The counter guy laughed. "Not that good; I just happened to have a whole one of those in my hands early this morning. Emmitt's Garage needed the assembly for a customer car."

"Many thanks," said Don and Rick as they headed out to visit Felix at Emmitt's. They both knew him. No surprise that patrol cars weren't always treated well in their day-to-day use. Emmitt's happened to be the shop that the campus police and the sheriff's department trusted for all their alignment work. They walked right into Felix's alignment bay when they got there. He was working on a beautiful 1969 Chevelle. Felix was also the go-to alignment guy for the local hot-rod shops.

"Hi guys," Felix said as they walked up. "Smash any more cruisers for me this week?" He laughed.

"Not yet, but we're always working on it," said Rick Walker, also laughing.

"Felix," Don said, holding up the evidence bag with the lens. "Does this look familiar?"

"Sure does. I swapped out a taillight assembly just this morning that should match that perfectly. It's over there in the plastic recycling bin."

Rick and Don followed Felix across the shop, where he produced the light assembly. It was missing a little more than Don's piece, but what they had fell into place as a perfect match. "Bingo!" said Don. "Whose car did this come from?"

"I don't know," said Felix. "But Theresa certainly will. She handles the customers."

"Can we keep this?" asked Don.

"Absolutely," replied Felix. "It's trash to us."

And Theresa did know. The vehicle in question belonged to James Giles.

"I think your puzzle piece just fell into place," said Rick.

They headed back to Don's office and called Shane Mitchell to report the day's news. He said he'd be joining them in the morning. He had new information from the review of Glenn's computer. He had also secured a warrant for a full search of Isabel's house, and he wanted to be there to check the new "James" thread as well. They'd start again as a threesome at 9:00 a.m. Tuesday.

TUESDAY MORNING

News from Harrisburg

Shane was in Don's office at 9:00 a.m. Tuesday as promised. He had grabbed half a dozen Egg McMuffins on the way to go with the coffee. Eat and sleep whenever you can in this job.

Rick and Don fielded questions about what they had found yesterday. Shane wasn't trying to grill them, Lieutenant Mitchell had just made it a career habit to recap early and often to make sure everyone stayed on the same page. "So," Shane said. "We confirmed what we knew about Weaver's cancer. I think Dr. Ryan and Dr. Frost will be writing a paper on that one. They were quite excited to get the scan from a month and a half ago. The tumor of concern had grown more than half a centimeter since then. We have a warrant for Isabel Helms' residence, so that's in the cards for today. There's a new twist there that I'll share in a minute. Based on interviews at YCCC and the research on the lens Don found at our fire site, we also have a more than probable James for some questioning. Am I missing anything from your travels yesterday?"

Rick answered first this time. "That covers us, I think. You indicated yesterday that you might have something from Glenn Weaver's computer."

"Yes, that's the new twist, and it's quite significant. Our hacker guys had no difficulty at all with the computer we took from the house at the barn fire scene. Our perp didn't seem to care if anyone found anything at all. He had a Microsoft Operating System and used the default browser; he did use a VPN, but no special firewalls and no exotic passwords. The techs loaded the COFEE software and picked it clean in less than an hour."

"To find?" Don said this time.

"There was a ton of expected stuff like art queries, pottery techniques, art supplies, and cannabis growing, all in line with what we already knew about Glenn."

"And?"

"Glenn had most recently spent time on a site called Xnorml. It's a portal for porn. It also has chat rooms and other means for like-minded users to share content and even meet."

"Now that surprises me," Don said. "I knew he was a little weird, but I would never have taken him for a pervert."

"We don't think he was, but we do have evidence of stalking. Glenn Weaver only recently registered the name 'Ironmansdungeon' on the site. In his first time on the Xnorml site, he initiated contact with a female user who went by '50shadesofunicorn.' 50shadesofunicorn was a pseudonym for Isabel Helms. In correspondence over several days, two weeks ago, the two exchanged messages, ultimately setting up a meeting for Friday, a week ago. Ironman said he would send a car, indicating the potential of an accomplice. Her iPad and phone went with her."

That news decided that the trio would begin their day at the home of Isabel Helms. Shane had already prepared for that, enlisting two of the lab technicians from Harrisburg to join them there. Everyone was assembled by 10:30 a.m. Don broke his seal and let the group in the front door. Shane was now in charge.

Addressing the technicians, Shane said, "This house is yours for the day and longer if you need it. It's already been searched superficially twice. There's no smoking gun that we know of here, but I want you to approach it as a fresh and very thorough crime scene investigation. I expect you to go through every closet, every door, and every page of every book. Don, Rick, and I will head straight to the garage to check one unopened item of interest. After that, we'll be off to several other leads. If you finish here today, seal everything back up and head back to Harrisburg with whatever you find. Everyone got that?" Nodding heads confirmed. "Then, let's glove up and get to work."

Don opened the garage for Shane and Rick to join him. Don had brought a chisel and hammer to dislodge the hasp with the attached padlock. It turned out to be mounted with simple, self-tapping wood screws and surrendered quickly. They saw an array of hanging clothes and opened the two doors on the bottom of the cabinet to find several loose items in one and lingerie in the other.

"50 shades for real," commented Rick Walker.

Shane called for one of the techs to join the group before they did anything else. With the potential for DNA collection, he wanted to make sure everything was handled correctly, fully witnessed, and properly packaged. The other tech continued his work inside the house. The loose items represented a variety of BDSM equipment, along with several unique vibrators and basic sex toys. Several pairs of handcuffs were removed first. These were especially likely to contain trace DNA other than Isabel's. Two ball gags were also similarly attractive as evidence. They were followed by the vibrators and other toys.

The lingerie drawer was next. This was well beyond the standard Victoria's Secret catalog. Crotchless panties and other cutout items abounded. The sheer fabrics would leave little to the imagination. This drawer also contained soft whips and bags of feathers. The hanging clothes were almost as revealing as the lingerie, including dresses with additional cutouts, high hems, and deep necklines. There were also costumes in various themes and a variety of leather, spandex, and rubber wear.

By 11:30, the three lead investigators had seen all they needed. They left the lab techs to their work on the scene. Don had James Giles' address from his personnel files. They would attempt to contact him there next. Chief Don Weston knew James well in his past role at the school. Dr. Giles' home was a nondescript end-unit townhouse. The condition and yard were neat and clean. The grass was green, but there were no trees, no shrubs, no flowers, no landscaping of any kind. Don went to the door alone while Rick and Shane stayed in the car. They were hoping to have him voluntarily come to the Sheriff's Office for questioning. A familiar face was their best bet for that.

At 12:30 p.m., the house erupted with wild barking when Don rang the doorbell. He heard a voice raised over the din, apparently trying to quiet the dog. About thirty seconds passed before James Giles opened the door to a spartan interior. The furniture was minimal and functional rather than comfortable looking. The only wall decoration visible from the doorway was a large cross over the fireplace mantel. "Don, what a surprise," he said. "Would you like to come in? I've sent noisy Sampson to his room." He laughed.

"Good to see you, James. No, I'll pass on the gracious invite, but I would like to ask you for a favor."

"Sure, Don, what is it?"

"I suppose it's no secret that we've had some unusual and tragic events surrounding Churchville University in the past week or so."

"Really?" said James. He laughed again. "Just kidding; I've seen the news. I feel terrible for Elly Olson. What a horrible thing. And just last night they said that nice Glenn Weaver had also passed away after the fire at his place. I can't imagine what you've been dealing with."

"It's been a messy situation for sure. We still have a lot of loose ends to pull together, which leads me to my request. Could I ask you to come to the County Sheriff's Office, possibly this afternoon or tomorrow morning? You're most familiar with the university leadership role, and you had some acquaintance with both men. There may be things you can help us understand about faculty relationships and school procedures. It could be very helpful to us."

"I suppose I would be your best source on college leadership. I can't come this afternoon. I have a paper that I'm involved in and need to get back to. What time tomorrow?"

"Would 10:00 tomorrow morning fit your schedule?" Don asked.

"I can do that."

"Do you know where the County Sheriff's Office is located?"

"I assume it would be the one on State Street?"

"That's it. I'll meet you there tomorrow, looking forward to catching up again. Thanks, James."

"Thank you, Don. Sorry about the trouble the school is having."

"Done," said Don as he got back in the car with Shane and Rick. "10:00 a.m. tomorrow."

"Good job," said Shane. "Let's do something portable for lunch. We can take it back to your office to regroup."

TUESDAY AFTERNOON

Jersey Mike's subs followed them back to the campus. Don was already thinking there'd be no dinner later; he had maxed out his calorie count for the day with this and the McMuffins. The large Dr. Pepper and chips wouldn't help either.

Shane began, "Thanks to you, Don, we may solve our James mystery tomorrow."

"Unless he talks to a lawyer, in which case he'll be a no-show for sure," said Rick.

"Of course," Shane said. "It's possible he's not Glenn's James, in which case he'd have nothing to be concerned about."

"Well," Don said. "James Giles is a very smart guy, and don't doubt that. His history, as I've witnessed it, is that he forms his own versions of things, doesn't seek counsel or want feedback, and rarely, if ever, questions his vision. He's probably right more than he's wrong, but if he is Glenn's James, he may be very wrong this time. Still, I'd bet he'll be there."

"That's a concern for tomorrow," Shane said. "Let's talk today. Knowing what we now seem to know about Isabel's social interests, it's hard to think that no one in her life ever had the slightest suspicion. Don, is there anyone on campus we can talk to who may have been close to her at all? You mentioned her administrative assistant and a teacher who told you about her poetry interest. Could either one of them possibly know more?"

"I don't think so, Shane, but I have given this a lot of thought, and I keep coming back to another source. The Olsons have known her for years before her arrival at Churchville and seemed to have at least some limited social connection. That, and the keys we've been using to access Isabel's house were given to me by Elly Olson. I don't think you give your house keys to someone you don't know and trust."

"First, let's finish lunch," said Shane. "And talk through our leads again versus our hard evidence and what we think we know. Then, we should probably see if Mrs. Olson is home and available to see us."

Shane continued, "I got a text message from our lab techs. They've wrapped up things at Isabel's house; nothing new since this morning. I re-directed them with the coordinates for Glenn's house. It's still on lockdown by one of Rick's officers as an active crime scene. The specific target there is the stun gun. So far, based on the knife and the blood types, Glenn likely had some involvement in the killing of Olson. Wait a minute. Don, do you have video footage that would place Glenn in the auditorium?"

"I do, and I certainly should have thought of that long before now. I was specifically looking for Harry's path, so I started my review by picking up time stamps on Friday afternoon. There is only one camera on the main auditorium entry. It won't take long to fast forward through that."

The camera showed Glenn entering the auditorium through the main door at 10:37 a.m. on Friday. "Can we go back further?" asked Rick. The Thursday footage had Glenn entering the building several times with various materials and equipment. It also showed him exiting each time.

"Did you find an entry or exit for Glenn on Saturday?" Shane asked.

"No," replied Don. "But the downstairs security door off the stage has no camera on it. All the auditorium doors were secured from the inside with angle iron and crossbeams welded to the door frames. The downstairs one was the only one secured from the outside, so it had to be the assailant's, or assailant's, point of exit. No other entries to the building appear on Saturday at any time. Glenn, or anyone else for that matter, could have entered and exited through that basement door."

"Agreed," said Shane. "If the guys can find the stun gun at Glenn's place, that will link him to both weapons believed to be used in the killing. DNA will be in tomorrow. If it matches the two bodies, as we expect it will, that will complete the picture of Glenn and Olson.

We still have Isabel and James in play. We'll talk to James tomorrow morning. Let's go see what Mrs. Olson can tell us about Isabel."

At 3:00 p.m. Tuesday, the three men set out across campus to the president's house.

THE ELLY INTERVIEW

On the way to see Elly, they stopped in at the open auditorium. The main doors had already been sent out for replacement matching. Twelve-foot tall and three-inch thick oak doors are not off-the-shelf items. It would be months before they could be re-created and installed.

The curtains on the stage were open. The only unusual signs were the side-door openings, closed with tarps. Maintenance crews had cleaned the hardwood planks on the stage floor. There was no envy for the folks who had that task. Before the end of the week, they'd likely have the stains sanded away and everything refinished. The damaged door frames had been removed with the doors. Replacements were on the way. The platform lift had been pushed to one side, awaiting parts. Vice grips were clamped on the hose to stop the fluid seepage.

Don, Rick, and Shane wandered the scene pensively, remembering the sights from only two days ago. The investigation seemed to have Glenn, if he was the figure in black, alone with Harry Olson at the time of the killing. A motive, however, was not entirely clear. The Weaver suicide would have already been a closed case based on the note and the knife. Instead, it was inextricably tied to their murder investigation. The knife had only complicated the Olson death and the missing person case of Isabel Helms. The DNA would likely settle that soon. But where was Isabel? And was the James of note truly James Giles?

Elly answered the door at the bell ring. It was immediately obvious that she was better rested and coming to grips with her husband's death. The presence of the children no doubt provided some comfort, and Ethan McCallum was always close by.

"Elly," said Don as they went again to sit in the living room. "You may remember Detective Rick Walker from the County Sheriff's Department. This is Lieutenant Shane Mitchell from the Pennsylvania State Police Bureau. He's the principal investigator covering our two deaths and the disappearance of Isabel Helms."

Shane led with empathy, "Mrs. Olson, I'm sorry we have to meet under such difficult circumstances. I've come to know a lot about your husband in the past few days. He was certainly a remarkable and well-respected man, and his passing is a great loss."

Harold Jr. and Cindy Olson had joined the group. "Thank you for that, Lieutenant," Elly responded. "Everyone, from Don to Ethan and in between, has been very kind and helpful. Of course, having the children with me now is the greatest comfort. This has all been the worst nightmare since Isabel disappeared, and then Harry." Tears now started, and Harold Jr. and Cindy Olson moved closer to their mom. Sobbing openly, Elly managed to choke out, "Do you think we'll ever know what happened to Isabel?"

Shane continued, "We're hoping you can help us with that question. It seems you and Dr. Olson may have been closer to Isabel Helms than anyone on campus. Would you agree with that?"

"Well, we've been friends with Isabel since we were together at Addison University. Harry and Isabel have regular tennis matches every week. Sometimes, the three of us would chat afterward. Isabel and I probably had lunch together every other week, maybe dinner if Harry was traveling or tied up with other school functions. We even took a couple of girls' weekends together—nothing unusual, just friends."

"And you had keys to Isabel's house. It would seem you were very good friends."

"I'd check on her plants if she was away and maybe return a book I had borrowed or drop off something she needed from the office."

"We were at Dr. Helms's house this morning and discovered a wardrobe cabinet with some unusual contents. Would you know anything about that?"

Elly turned to Chief Weston. "Don, can you stop this?"

"It's important, Elly. It may help us to find Isabel."

"Kids, can you start getting something for dinner together? We'll be done here soon." Harold Jr. and Cindy Olson left the living room. They seemed to register that the next part of the conversation was not for them.

Elly asked, "What is your interest in this cabinet?"

Shane replied, "Are you aware of it?"

"Yes, Isabel kept some girly things there. A grown, single woman can have girly things, can't she?"

Shane continued, "Certainly, she can, Mrs. Olson. There's absolutely nothing wrong with Dr. Helms possessing the things we found there. I was just trying to establish if you knew about them and could verify that they belonged to her. Thank you for confirming both. Let's move on. We have some evidence that links Isabel Helms through some correspondence with Glenn Weaver. Do you know of any prior relationship between those two?"

Elly laughed out loud, which seemed an odd response. "Isabel never would have had a relationship with him. She was an absolute first-class act, and he was just another faculty member that wouldn't have been an attraction to any self-respecting woman."

"I'm sorry, Mrs. Olson," Shane continued. "I didn't mean to imply a relationship of a personal nature. I was wondering if you might be aware of any work-related connections. Dr. Helms and Dr. Olson were the academic leaders of Churchville University. When Detective Walker was conducting faculty interviews last Thursday, several faculty members expressed discomfort about job security and even suggested that a 'purge' of faculty was occurring. Were you aware of anything that might have been causing some faculty discomfort?"

"Everything causes faculty discomfort," she said harshly. "They don't know anything about the business of running a college. I've been by Harold's side as he has dedicated his life to college leadership and how to do it right. All faculty do is complain. Most of them are overpaid drains that should be 'purged,' if that's what they want to call it. Something must go when the university is bleeding money. To answer your question, yes, I know that retirements and generous severances were being offered to some of the teachers. What's wrong with that?"

"Nothing at all," Shane said. "Our business must fit into budget constraints as well, and it's never easy, especially when it involves personnel. Would you happen to know if Glenn Weaver was part of the group that was going to be displaced?"

"I know that Harry has that file on his desk. He's agonized over it for months. Would you like to see it?"

"I would, and I'd like to make a copy if that's possible. It may be very useful to our investigation."

Elly got up and Don Weston said, "Let me help you, Elly. I don't think we'll have any more questions, will we, Lieutenant?"

"No, Chief Weston," Shane said. "If you can help Mrs. Olson with a copy of that file, we'll be done here."

The IT department had fully equipped Harold's home office exactly as all administrative offices on campus. Don was able to quickly scan the five-page document. "Elly," Chief Weston said as they were alone in the office. "Out of my respect for you and Harry, I didn't want to ask this in front of our guests, but it needs to be asked. There are potential consequences if you are not fully and completely honest with me on this. Did Harry have a relationship with Isabel that went beyond their jobs at the school?" Elly said nothing as her eyes filled up and tears began to overflow.

The silence continued for twenty seconds, which seemed like an hour until Don broke the void, "Elly, if you aren't fully and completely honest with me at this moment, your next interview will be a formal one at the sheriff's office." More tears and a choking sob escaped Elly's lips. "I promise that what you tell me now will be held with the strictest confidence and discretion possible. Did Harry have a relationship with Isabel that went beyond their jobs at the school?"

"Yes," she said. "And so did I."

"Were these sexual relationships?"

"Yes," she said haltingly through more tears and sobs. "And much more than that; they were very special friendships."

"In our investigation, we keep coming back to a link with an internet site called Xnorml. Is that something that you and Harold and Isabel engaged with?"

"No, Harry and I were aware of Isabel's other interests, but we only experienced that through what she shared with us. It wasn't an attraction we were drawn to." Elly continued, now composed, seeming to be relieved to release a burden and secrets that she feared had contributed to the recent events. "Isabel, Harold, and I have been friends and lovers for many years. Our relationships have always been open and non-judgmental, based only on our love for each other. I know our chosen arrangements are not usual or expected in a marriage, or responsible careers, but the three of us never questioned the genuine affection we had for each other and had a great appreciation for the serendipity that joined us."

Don said, "In the years that the three of you were in a relationship, have there ever been disagreements or issues that complicated or clouded things for any of you, or all of you?"

"Never! Don, I understand that a spouse or lover will always be a suspect in a murder, but the relationship the three of us had was one of no possessiveness or jealousy ever. We all enjoyed our company and pleasure together and only wished the same for each partner. Harold and I practiced an open marriage from the beginning. Our outside activities were always superficial until Isabel joined us. Since then, I have always felt complete and fulfilled. Right now, I've never felt so empty and alone."

"Elly, thank you for being honest with me. I had to hear that, and I hope we can let this conversation stay between us."

"Thank you, Don, for being gentle with me. I know this is hard for both of us."

When Don and Elly returned to the living room with Harry's notes, Don again thanked Elly, told her she had been very helpful, and collected the other two investigators on his way out of the house.

BACK AT THE CAMPUS POLICE OFFICE

The file from President Olson's desk was a spreadsheet of all the Churchville faculty. Don Weston made additional copies for the other two investigators, and they all set in to decipher the pages.

Categories were listed as "tenured," "tenure track," "full time," and "adjunct." Beside each name were columns for salary, time of service, terminal degree, and separation date. The next two columns were labeled severance and meeting date, and the last had no heading. It was for special notes. Almost two-thirds of the total faculty meetings had already taken place. All but a few of the tenured had pending meeting dates noted. About fifteen percent of that group had the "severance" box checked with a separation date of May 31. Several of those had special notes of "package negotiation," presumably in President Olson's handwriting.

The tenure track names had few concluded meeting dates. Two that did, had "severance" checked with no special notes. A handful of others that had no meeting date were already marked in special notes for 'tenure denial pending' in the same handwriting. The 'severance' ones had the same May 31 separation date. The full-time list was especially active. Most meetings had already taken place. A third of these names had no separation date, presumably surviving the purge. Of the ones that did have the May 31 end of career, only about half had a check in the "severance" column. The rest read simply "no."

Glenn Weaver was in the full-time category as a visiting professor. His meeting date had already occurred. His time would end on May 31. He had no severance package.

Detective Rick Walker spoke first. "If we had this list when we were interviewing faculty last week, we could have been way better focused. The no-severance separations would have been our first targets. We would likely have talked to Glenn Weaver before the Saturday events."

"No question," said Don. "I knew the faculty seemed to be having some issues, but I certainly didn't know the scope of this. Knowing what we know now, and coupling that with Weaver's cancer, you could certainly start making a case for motive."

"I'd buy that," said Lieutenant Shane Mitchell. "Well, it's almost 5:00. I packed a bag to stay over; does anyone have a hotel suggestion?"

"Stay with me," Don said. "I have an empty house with three extra rooms. I'd like the company."

"Maybe I can buy us a great steak dinner tonight," said Shane. "I'd like to pick your brain some more. I may technically be the lead on these cases, but it's your 'ground zero.' Plus, you probably have more total law enforcement experience than Rick and I combined. I can always learn something new."

"While you two are bromancing," said Rick. "I'm going home to my wife and kids. Who knows what tomorrow will bring? I'll see you at the Sheriff's Office, 9:00-ish, tomorrow."

"We know tomorrow will bring James Giles for one," said Shane. "Oh, and DNA should be in tomorrow. Speaking of DNA, I had another text from Travis. He and Jerome are taking a melted hunk of something back with them from Glenn's barn, possibly our stun gun."

Rick gave a thumbs up on the way out the door.

"Shane, I need to make one phone call before we head out," said Don. He called Alvin Corson at WYCC. "Alvin, I want to thank you for whatever you're doing to keep the out-of-town wolves at bay. I haven't seen one camera, and I haven't gotten a single call."

"That's good to hear, Don. I'm not sure I have any control over that. How has your work gone since we talked yesterday morning? Anything you can share?"

"We have surfaced some additional evidence that adds to the investigation. We should have our DNA profiles back tomorrow, and we expect to pull much of that together. Will that buy us another day if you report it?"

"It may. Do you have any news on the missing woman?"

"Not that I'd like to see on TV. Can I ask you to continue that as just a missing person scenario?"

"Certainly. I appreciate what you just gave me, and I'll look to hear from you tomorrow on the DNA."

"Thanks, Alvin. I owe you another lunch." He hung up. "Done here," Don said to Shane. "Let's get you settled into your lodging."

TUESDAY EVENING

Don Weston willingly and unashamedly went way over his calorie limit Tuesday. On top of McDonald's breakfast, Jersey Mike's lunch, and a couple of full-sugar soft drinks, he added 1,987 calories of steak, mushrooms, baked potato, Caesar salad, and half a bottle of red wine that he split with Shane.

Over dinner, Shane Mitchell picked Don's brain as promised. Don had been at Churchville for five years. That was a very Mayberry type of police experience compared to the thirty-plus years he had on the Philadelphia Police Force. Shane opened with, "So, what was it like all those years in the City of Brotherly Love?"

Don laughed. "Back in the last century, in the '80s, when you would probably have been an infant, I was turned out as a fresh graduate from the academy. At that time, urban police work anywhere was neither brotherly nor loving. Every big city still had lingering memories of the '60s riots and the protests of the '70s. Crack hit in the '80s and overwhelmed everything."

"How did you come to know Lester Timmons?"

"That came later. As I made my way in the streets to detective, corporal, sergeant, and lieutenant, I was fortunate to stay out of trouble and get some good cases. By the time I became captain, I was asked to head our inter-departmental communication and task force. That put me in a position to work with every department in and around the city, including SEPTA, the military, and the FBI field offices. Naturally, the surrounding counties in Pennsylvania, New Jersey, and Delaware and the State Police were also key partners. That's when Lester and I hit it off."

"Any favorite cases in your years on the street?"

"Not really, but I did have some involvement with a string of unrelated mass murders that hit the city in the 80's. Two of the killers, Garry Heidnik and Harrison Graham, were operating at the same time. Heidnik was known as the Ted Bundy of Philadelphia. He kidnapped and tortured at least six women. Graham was dubbed the House of Death killer. He had the bodies of seven women in his apartment when we arrested him."

Shane jumped in, "I know both of those from my undergrad, law enforcement, and college days. Wasn't there also a Frankford Slasher at the same time?"

"Yes. That one carried into the mid-90s. It's especially bothersome because it's still unsolved."

"That's some wicked stuff," said Shane. "I can't say I've personally encountered any mass murderers."

"Yet," said Don, laughing. "That could change this week."

"Yikes, I wasn't thinking of that." Shane went on, "I know from Lester that you had private consulting relationships with many departments before and since leaving Philadelphia. He says you're the go-to guy for advice on best practices in crime-scene investigation and evidence handling, public relations, and, more recently, campus security."

"I've heard that," said Don, laughing again. "But enough about me. What are you having for dessert? Care to split a bread pudding?"

Shane felt very fortunate to get some private time in Don's company.

Don thought of Helen as he lay in bed that night. "Helen, I ate too much again."

You've got a lot on your mind. You can always recover from a few extra calories later.

"A week ago, I was frustrated and bored and thinking about quitting. Now I don't know which way to turn. Three friends are gone suddenly, probably all dead. I know in my gut it's all related, but I'm having a hard time imagining why."

You've got a lot of good colleagues to help you.

"I do, but somehow I feel alone in the responsibility to work things out and find a solution."

You're not alone, there are a lot of us with you.

"I think what hurts the most is I might have been able to save Dr. Olson if I hadn't been wallowing in my pity."

You have to let that go, Don. We know that things happen for a reason and people go when they're supposed to. You'll find the answers. You always do.

"Thanks, Helen, love you"

Don drifted off to a sound sleep.

WEDNESDAY

Is this THE James?

Campus Police Chief Don Weston and Lieutenant Shane Mitchell joined Detective Rick Walker at the York County Sherriff's Office on Wednesday at 9:00 a.m. Everyone was well-rested and in good spirits.

"You boys get any sleep last night?" asked Rick. "I know I had a good eight hours."

Shane responded, "Slept great. I had a lot to learn from Don's history lesson. Did you know he single-handedly captured Ted Bundy and invented Post-It notes at the same time?"

"Umm, no, I wasn't aware of that. That must have been after he took down John Wilkes Booth and invented the internet."

"Actually," said Don. "That was Day Seven; I was resting then. I thought you guys would be better at getting your facts straight."

"Speaking of facts," Shane said. "DNA profiles should be completed sometime this morning. More trace DNA work is pending on the articles from Isabel Helms' wardrobe cabinet, probably nothing useful there. The thing our evidence techs found in the wood stove at the barn may or may not have been our stun gun. The melted plastic and wiring were consistent with such a weapon, and it did have batteries, which exploded in the fire. It's destroyed. They're trying to identify a similar weapon that would match the component remnants, starting from the information Rick gave us on his magic wand."

Today's DNA news was expected to confirm the identities of the blood on the knife found at the barn fire. There was little doubt it would positively match the two dead bodies.

Shane continued, "We expect James Giles here at 10:00. We'll have Officer Friendly Don meet him. I'll be waiting in the interrogation room. I just met Sheriff Bill Hester when we were coming in. Rick, Bill said he'd be joining you behind the mirror."

Detective Rick Walker said, "That's good; I owe him an update on how his county resources are being spent on this investigation anyway."

James Giles pulled up in his Subaru wagon precisely at 10:00 and was greeted in the parking lot by Don Weston. Chief Weston couldn't help but notice the shiny, clean, right rear taillight on Giles' vehicle. They chatted briefly about the old days at Churchville as they entered the building and went to the assigned room. Everyone else was already in place. Don made introductions, "James, this is Lieutenant Shane Mitchell from the Pennsylvania State Police Bureau. He's the principal investigator covering our two deaths." To Shane, he said, "James Giles was the former dean at Churchville University. I invited him here to fill in some blank spaces we may have on faculty relationships and school procedures."

Lieutenant Shane Mitchell began, "Very nice to meet you, Mr. Giles."

"That would be Dr. Giles."

"Sorry, of course. My apologies. I'm not very familiar with academic practices and courtesies. That's why your input is so valuable to us in the investigation."

"I understand and forgive you," James said, smiling.

Don asked if anyone needed coffee or water. "I'm getting a coffee myself," he said. Shane and James declined. Shane shuffled papers and didn't say a word in Don's absence. "Well, let's get started," Shane said upon Don's return. "Dr. Giles, can you tell us your current title?"

"I'm currently on loan to the Churchville University Mennonite community as the Director of Research and Chronicles. I'm also the Dean of Academics for Churchville University."

"I didn't realize that," said Don Weston. "I thought the new provost and division head structure had changed that position."

"That's a fairly common error, Don," said James. "But the Dean of Academics is a lifetime position. The president of the university bestowed that title on me, and it remains my title until and unless I relinquish it. That's the university's history and precedent. I've been in contact with some of the board members, and I'm certain they'll be asking me back to that position very soon, as the university is without academic leadership currently."

"That's very interesting and helpful," said Shane. "Again, I'm unclear on the titles and structure of academia. How does that impact the provost position?"

"Under the circumstances, not at all. It's my understanding that the position has been vacated. It seems the provost has left the university and abandoned the office."

"That's news to us," Don chimed in.

"What can you tell us about the provost?" asked Shane.

"I don't know much about Ms. Helms—"

"That would be Dr. Helms," Shane interjected, triggering the "bad cop" role.

"Of course, thank you," James said. "I heard that Dr. Helms had left town a week or so ago."

Shane spoke again, "We knew she was missing but hadn't heard she was known to have left town. Did you hear that from Glenn Weaver?"

Wide eyes and a little fluster appeared this time before James said, "I don't know what you're talking about. Why would I hear anything from Glenn Weaver, of all people?"

"We had a conversation with Erin Eland at York County Community College," said Shane. "She indicated that you and Glenn spent quite a bit of time together recently at his art show there. Is that correct?"

A little more fluster was apparent. "I did stop in at his art show, but just to say hello."

"We found a note from Glenn," Shane piled on, "that ended with 'p.s. – Thank you James for being a friend at the end.' The note seems to have been written very shortly before Mr. Weaver died. Could that James be you?"

James was always in charge and suddenly not. His knuckles were turning white as he gripped the arms of the chair in a quickly rising rage and suddenly shifted to offense. His voice was raised almost to a shout as he sputtered out, "I am the dean of a university and a leader of the church. I will not have you disrespect that. You are trying to set me up in some fake theory of yours, and I'll have none of it." Turning to Don, he said, "Don Weston, you brought me here under false pretenses, and you should be ashamed of yourself." Turning back to Shane, he said, "I'm not listening to any more of this, and I'll be leaving now. Do not contact me again. If you think you're going to continue this in any way, you'll need to speak to my attorney, George Hunt."

"You're free to go," said Shane.

And just like that, James Giles left the building. Don and Shane joined Rick Walker and Bill Hester in Hester's office.

"Well, that went well," laughed Don.

"Too much, too soon?" said Shane.

"I don't think so," said Don. "I believe you read the room quite well, and I believe we have confirmed our James of interest. I think we did the right thing to hold back on the taillight evidence. No doubt it will come in handy when we meet again."

"I was hoping you'd say that," said Shane. "Are you familiar with his attorney, George Hunt?"

Don laughed again. "Quite familiar," he said. "We're very good friends. George and I are both amateur Civil War historians. He's also the past president of the university. He hired me, and he's the one who put James Giles into the dean position. Let's give our James the rest of the morning to think about things, and I'll call George this afternoon."

"Let's check on our DNA profiles," Shane said. "We may be putting out a press release this afternoon."

ALVIN CORSON

It was just after 11:00 a.m. when the DNA profile information came in. As thought, the body DNA and two blood samples from the knife confirmed Glenn Weaver and Harold Olson as the sources. The AB-positive blood sample from the knife was a match with the hair DNA previously collected from Isabel's home. Shane asked Don Weston to see if Alvin Corson was available for lunch. He was.

Don was always good at introductions. "Alvin, this is Lieutenant Shane Mitchell from the Pennsylvania State Police Bureau. He's the principal investigator covering our two deaths. Shane, this is Alvin Corson, the news anchor for WYCC in York."

"Good to meet you," said Shane. "Don thinks very highly of you as a journalist and a friend. I hope we can enjoy the same relationship."

"Any friend of Don's is a friend of mine. Glad to meet you as well." Turning to Don, Alvin asked, "Good news, I hope?"

Chips and salsa arrived, and orders were placed. "Alvin," Don said, "there's no good news anywhere in this case, but there is news that needs to be reported, and we're trusting you to help us with that."

"That's easy, Don; it's what I do. I know you were expecting some DNA work. I'm guessing it came in?"

"Yes," said Don. "It confirmed some things we thought we knew. There are some new items of confirmed news for you to report. There are also some things I didn't tell you before that are part of that. A knife was found at the fire scene at Glenn Weaver's barn. It was a source of the DNA we received today."

"Can I report now that Glenn Weaver's death was a suicide and release the note?"

"You can confirm it as a suspected suicide and share the note."

"Done," said Corson. "What else?"

"I'll let Shane give you the complete news story. It's his investigation."

"Alvin," said Shane. "You might want to keep some notes."

"Is it okay if I record our conversation?"

"Don has told me you're a trusted ally and I'm good with that, but I'd prefer we keep to notes for now. I hope you understand."

"I do, and I'm all yours."

Lunch arrived. "First off, we appreciate how you've worked with Don on information control, especially with other news outlets. We've been able to carry on the investigation without interference, and that's always valuable. After your news report tonight, I don't think that will be the case. For the record, please list me as the chief investigator, Lieutenant Shane Mitchell from the Pennsylvania State Police Bureau. I work under the office of Lieutenant Colonel Lester Timmons, Director of the Pennsylvania State Police Bureau of Criminal Investigation based in Harrisburg. We need you to direct any leads or inquiries to that office, here's the phone number. They have the resources to work with the press. Your story tonight will be an exclusive, but the Harrisburg office will confirm it with a press release by 11:00 p.m."

"Thank you, Lieutenant, I appreciate your confidence in me. We'll lead tonight with the confirmation of the suspected Weaver suicide. Should I reference the knife?"

"Alvin," Don this time. "No, not yet. This is where it gets complicated. We also want you to follow up on the missing person case of Dr. Isabel Helms and make another appeal for public information on her whereabouts. Between you and us, and this is in strictest confidence, the knife contains a possible blood match for her as well. We still have not found her, but we now have potential evidence of foul play in her disappearance."

"And some link to Glenn Weaver, at least," said Corson.

"Correct, Alvin," said Shane. "But all we want you to report on is the suicide confirmation, the missing person appeal, and what we can share from the suicide note. You can report all of that. Don will send you a photo link of a portion of the note. It says, 'p.s. – Thank you James for being a friend at the end.' We're looking for the public's help in identifying who James is. We do have a person of interest. You can report all of that. And again, refer all leads and inquiries to Harrisburg."

"How about the cause of death for Harold Olson? I assume Glenn died in the fire."

"Glenn did die in the fire. The cause of death for Dr. Olson was asphyxiation."

"Strangled?"

"Hanging, but let's leave it at asphyxiation for now. I don't believe our person of interest knows the exact method."

"Is your person of interest someone named James?"

"It would be nice if your news story just said, 'person of interest that may have some more information.' This person is not necessarily a suspect."

"Okay," Corson said. "The story is the Olson cause of death, that Glenn Weaver's death is suspected to be a suicide, Isabel Helms is still a missing person, and Harold Olson's cause of death was asphyxiation. Motive is still unknown?"

"Correct," said Shane.

Referring to his notes, Alvin Corson asked, "How will this be? We have some updates to our ongoing, exclusive coverage of the recent events surrounding Churchville University. The cause of death for President Harold Olson is listed as asphyxiation. Additional details are pending. Visiting art professor Glenn Weaver appears to have killed himself in a fire set in his barn. A suicide note was found at the scene with an unknown reference to someone named James. A person of interest has been identified that police hope can provide further information. That person's name has not been released, and they are not considered a suspect at this time.

"The missing persons case of Dr. Isabel Helms, the University provost, is still an ongoing police investigation. If you at home know of anything that can help the police solve the identity of James or details in the missing person case, please direct all contact to the office of Lieutenant Colonel Lester Timmons, director of the Pennsylvania State Police Bureau of Criminal Investigation based in Harrisburg. The chief investigator for this case is Lieutenant Shane Mitchell from the Pennsylvania State Police Bureau. Are you good with that, Shane, to put all of that out?"

"I think you nailed it. Any other thoughts, Don?"

"Perfect," said Don Weston.

"If it's okay with you, Don," said Shane. "I'd like to stay over at your place another night. I think this will generate some interest, and there are a couple of things we may need to think about in the morning."

"No problem, Shane," said Don. "I enjoy having some company. Alvin, thanks again. We'll let you know what happens next."

JAMES AND GEORGE

James drove straight from the Sheriff's Office to the Law Offices of Hunt and Hutchison. George Hunt and Webster Hutchison had been partners for over forty years. The firm was just the two of them plus one legal assistant who had been there almost thirty years, Sandra Thornton. Their specialty was business law, from incorporation to forensic accounting. They purposely kept the business small, maintaining a solid income with a loyal following in the area.

George Hunt's twenty years as Churchville University president had not been an interruption at all to their success.

James Giles was not happy and hit the door hard on his way in. "I need to see George Hunt immediately," he said, a little loudly.

Sandra Thornton was at her desk in the foyer. She was a very even-keeled woman. Sandra knew James from George Hunt's Churchville days. James's urgency was rude at best, but Sandra sought to defuse it with her usual Southern charm. "Dr. Giles, it's been ages. How are you?" she said politely.

"Frankly, I'm not sure how I am now. I need to speak to George."

"Well, the partners are in conference right now, but let me go check and see if George can break away to see you."

Sandra disappeared through a large wooden door to the conference room. George and Webster were there, discussing local sports while enjoying a lunch of pastrami and corned beef sandwiches from the local deli. "George, I'm sorry to interrupt, but James Giles is here. He's quite insistent that he needs to see you right away."

George said, "Well, I suppose that could be more interesting than Webster's faulty take on the demise of the Churchville baseball team.

Put him in my office, and I'll be there shortly. Sorry, Webster, I'll be back to correct you soon." George laughed.

Sandra moved James to the office, where he waited briefly. There was a lot of Churchville University memorabilia there to look at. James wanted to get this mess over with so he could get back to his own office on campus again. He had been away from the university for too long, and there were many things in the works there that needed to be fixed.

"James," George said as he entered the office. "What a pleasure to see you." He gave him a handshake on his way to the big leather chair. "How have you been?"

"Not so good, George," he said, tightlipped. "I think I need a lawyer."

"That's very convenient; I happen to be one," George laughed. "What is your legal need?"

"I've just come from the Sheriff's Office, and it seems they think I have something to do with the death of Glenn Weaver. And Don Weston was in on it, too. He made me come there on false pretenses."

George paused briefly to consider that. "Well, that's certainly interesting to hear. Do you have anything to do with the death of Glenn Weaver?" he asked with a light smile.

"Of course not," James answered sharply.

"Then, what is your concern? You can tell me anything, and I assure you it will be a private conversation."

"George, I think it's very important that you and I return to Churchville University right away. They have no academic leadership and no direction, and we can help get the school back on track."

"James, neither of us have any role there anymore." George Hunt wasn't smiling now.

"Yes, we do. You're the president and I'm the dean."

"James, that's been a couple of years."

"But it doesn't end. The Academic Dean is a lifetime position."

"I'm not sure I ever understood that to be the case, James."

"In the history of the university, it has always been a lifetime position. The Academic Dean is the leader of the university until they choose to step down. You may have decided to leave as president, but I never stepped down from my post. I always knew I'd be coming back, and the university needs me to come back now."

"James, the academic structure of the university has changed since then. I don't want to debate whether a position belongs to an individual for life, but the position of dean no longer exists anyway."

"Don't you see that the current president is gone, and the provost has abandoned her post? They need us now."

"Oh? I knew about the misfortune with President Olson. What are you referring to with the provost?"

"She has left town and isn't coming back."

"I hadn't heard that, but I'm sure if they have a real need, Stewart Mason, as the school's legal counsel, can step in to keep things going as he has in the past. Let's get back to why you came here. Can you tell me how the police think you're involved in Glenn Weaver's death?"

"They said they had spoken to someone who saw me with him at an art exhibit recently. They also said his suicide note said something about, 'Thank you, James,' and they think I'm that James."

"I didn't know there was a suicide note. This whole situation has been very disconcerting. Is that possible he may have been referring to you?"

"I suppose," James answered quietly.

"Tell me about that. If you've done nothing wrong, you have nothing to worry about."

"I did stop in to see him at a show at YCCC. And we talked afterward."

"What did you talk about?"

"Did you know that Glenn was fired from the school?"

"No, but I did know that several faculty positions were being considered in cost cutting. I suppose he could have been one of those."

"Well, he was. He was cut off with no notice and no severance or insurance."

"That is bad news but not unusual for non-tenure separations. Why does the Glenn Weaver situation become a special concern for you?"

"He also found out recently that he has terminal cancer. He was very upset and angry. If I were there, he would still have a job."

"But he'd also still have terminal cancer. I suppose that would explain a suicide mentality. Did you know that was his plan?"

"No. I mean, he said his life was over, but I didn't think anything of it. I just knew he was angry at the whole situation, and I thought we may be able to do something about it."

"We, do you mean you and I, or you and Glenn?"

"Both. I believe very strongly that there has been something wrong with the relationship between the president and the provost. I knew it when they pushed me aside. Now, they were trying to change the entire university and it's not good. We had to do something."

"We again; do you mean you and I, or you and Glenn?"

"Both. You and I need to return to take control of the university situation before it is too late."

"And you and Glenn?"

"Glenn was going to help me find out about the president and the provost. Once everyone knew the truth, they would be removed, and things could go back to normal."

"So, what did you and Glenn hope to do?"

"We found out that Isabel Helms had a secret life as a prostitute."

"A prostitute?"

"Some sort of ungodly, sex thing with whips and masks."

"Fascinating," said George. "How did you find this information?"

"On her computer. Glenn found it."

"Her school computer?"

"No, she had an iPad."

"And she just gave you access to it?"

"No, Glenn went to her house while she was away."

"So, breaking and entering?"

"Glenn said the house was unlocked."

"James," George said, "I must stop you here. We just went into a criminal area and I'm not a criminal attorney. I think it would be wise if I don't hear any more. You're already admitting to knowledge of an unlawful entry at least, and it sounds like you may have had some questionable arrangement with a dead man. My recommendation is that we find you a criminal attorney to hear the whole story before you say anything else to me or the police. I'd also recommend that you let go of the thought of ever returning to the university. You and I don't belong there, and we haven't for some time." James had tears in his eyes and was silent. "Do you understand what I'm saying, James? I know a very good attorney that I would consider a specialist in this area. He could give you the best advice before things go any further. I think you need that right now."

Silence.

"His name is Vincent Reese. I can call him for you. Would you like me to do that?"

"I'd like everything to go back to normal."

THE EVENING NEWS

WYCC had been running promotions throughout the day, promising late-breaking developments in the Churchville University president's murder. It didn't disappoint for the communities of York, Churchville, and the larger viewing area.

Alvin Corson delivered right on the script; the story was told over images of the Churchville campus. He closed with, "This is certainly a great tragedy that has hit our usually quiet community very hard. I have worked with President Olson on several local events for the university. He came to Churchville several years ago when the university had a real need for fresh leadership, and he's been a respected addition to that historic institution. I've also worked with artist Glenn Weaver. His artwork and his metal sculptures are familiar to many of us in the area. He was an exceptionally talented and gifted craftsperson.

"I do not know Dr. Isabel Helms personally, but I've spoken with many of her colleagues. They have universally shared that she is a well-thought-of, excellent administrator. They are all hoping that she can still be found. Very sad news, indeed. Again, this is an active police investigation. If you at home know of anything that can help the police identify the reference in the suicide note or solve the missing person case, please direct all contact to the office of Lieutenant Colonel Lester Timmons, director of the Pennsylvania State Police Bureau of Criminal Investigation based in Harrisburg. The phone number is on your screen. Thank you."

THURSDAY

Ten Days from the Missing Person Report on Isabel Helms

Don Weston and Shane Mitchell had a big breakfast at the house and headed for Don's office at about 8:00 a.m. While they were reviewing tasks for the day, George Hunt called.

"Don, it's George. I get the impression you've had your hands full recently."

"You're a very perceptive man, George. It has been like the wrong side of Antietam over here for the past week or so. Good to hear from you."

"Always nice to catch up, but I don't prefer the circumstances this time."

"That makes two of us. If, and when, this ever ends, I need a road trip. I had to cut the annual Gettysburg weekend short. Could I talk you into a few nights up that way? Oh, and do you mind if I put you on speakerphone? I have Lieutenant Shane Mitchell here with me. He's the lead investigator on the case."

"You got it on Gettysburg when this ends. The speaker phone is fine. I suspect your visitor would benefit from the conversation. I had a visitor of my own yesterday that might be of interest to you."

"James Giles, I presume? I was going to check in with you this morning, but you beat me to it. Can you tell me about it?

"Not really. I told him our conversation would be private. I think it's okay to tell you he said that our missing provost has left town and isn't coming back. No doubt you would have already known that."

"No," said Don. "We don't know that, but Giles made a similar, odd statement to us. Thanks for telling me that."

"Oops," said George. "I have referred him to Vincent Reese for counsel; I believe you know him."

"I do; good and fair, criminal defense. I've used him in the past for perspective on some of our Title IX cases. So, you think James has some criminal involvement?"

"Let's just say I believe he wanted me to represent him, and our conversation reached a point where I would not be a help. He would likely gain more benefit from Vincent, and I contacted Reese on his behalf. They will be meeting at 9:00 this morning. After seeing last night's news coverage, I'm confident it was good advice."

Don chuckled. "Well, you've said a lot by saying little. Thanks for the heads up."

"Let me know if I can be of any help. I've been working with Harry Olson behind the scenes since he arrived here. I'm very familiar with the administrative changes at the university and the current faculty-thinning process." George Hunt had played his Harold Olson conversation over and over again in his head over the past week. He couldn't help but wonder if there was something in that genesis that had contributed to two deaths and a disappearance. "You know I have a love for the place, as you do, and it's all deeply disturbing. The missing provost only confounds the tragedy of the recent events. The university will miss Harry. He was doing a great job of getting things under control and poised for a better outlook."

"George, I understand and appreciate you. I'll ring you up on our Civil War trip soon."

"Thanks, Don. Best of luck on putting all the pieces together."

Don turned to Shane. "What do you like next?" he asked.

"I think we should visit with Mrs. Olson again."

ANYTHING ELSE YOU CAN TELL US?

Elly Olson seemed almost back to normal when she greeted Don Weston and Shane Mitchell at the door. She'd had the company of the kids for several days now, which helped immensely. She also had the confirmation of an unnatural death on campus, which triggered double indemnity on the university president's life insurance policy. That, and the Olson family resources, meant that she would be a very wealthy woman with no restrictions for the rest of her life. She was still a grieving widow, but the corresponding concerns of the next steps were erased by the financial assurance.

"You just missed Ethan McCallum," she said. "It seems like everyone is coming to check on me this morning. I suppose I owe that to last night's evening news."

"Yes, I suppose you do," said Don. "Elly, I'm sure you remember Lieutenant Shane Mitchell from the Pennsylvania State Police Bureau."

"I do, and I think I owe you an apology, Lieutenant Mitchell, for my outburst the other day."

"Not at all, Mrs. Olson. I believe you've been extremely patient and helpful. None of us are ever at their best in these circumstances."

"Please feel free to call me Elly. I guess you may have some more questions for me. Should we sit in the living room again? I just made some fresh lemonade. I'll join you there with three glasses."

When all were settled, Don started, "Elly, I want you to know that you are not considered a suspect in any of this. The questions we have involve some direct evidence from an apparent link between

Dr. Isabel Helms and Glenn Weaver. Anything you can tell us might help find out what has happened regarding Dr. Helms."

Tears issued forth from Elly. "I'm sorry, I thought I had it under control. Losing Isabel and Harry is beyond the worst thing I can imagine. And losing them this way is just so wrong."

"Elly, can I get you anything?" Don asked.

More tears followed. "I'm sorry for being like this. The only thing I want in the world is to see them again."

"I understand."

Shane started, "Elly, I know this is an uncomfortable territory, but we need to go back to the evidence that links Isabel Helms through some correspondence with Glenn Weaver. Are you familiar with a computer site called Xnorml?"

Elly looked at Don for direction. "Elly, I have not shared our private conversation. It's okay to answer the question." Shane looked at Don. "Trust me," Don said.

Elly answered, "I've heard of it, but I'm not personally familiar with it."

"It's a portal where people can meet and discuss different interests, mostly sexual. We believe Glenn Weaver contacted Dr. Helms anonymously on that site. Can you think of anything that might relate to that?"

"Isabel and I were very good friends, closer than sisters, and Harry, too. It was not unusual for us to share our thoughts and plans about anything. Isabel was here, sitting right where you are, just a week ago Friday, talking about the upcoming weekend. Harry and I were going to spend a quiet weekend, a drive in the country, nothing special. Isabel told us she had big plans for the weekend but nothing more. Does that help?"

"We believe that Isabel was meeting with Glenn Weaver on that Friday night."

Elly, triggered again, said, "I can assure you she would never have anything to do with Glenn Weaver or any other faculty member."

"She wouldn't have known at the time it was Mr. Weaver. Have you ever known her to have an anonymous meeting with anyone?"

Elly, crying now, responded, "I don't know what to say." More hesitation, another glance exchanged with Don, and then, quietly, "Yes, she sometimes met with people anonymously."

"The contents in the wardrobe found in her garage would be consistent with an interest in meetings of a sexual nature and possibly BDSM encounters. Are you familiar with the meaning of BDSM?"

"Yes, I am."

"That's not a crime, and we don't have any judgmental position on anyone's choices, but if it's related to a crime, we need to investigate it. Do you know if Dr. Helms had any interest or experience with a BDSM lifestyle? And could that possibly relate to any of her anonymous encounters? I know those are hard questions, but it could be very important."

Very quietly, Elly said, "She did have that interest and, yes, she had met others anonymously in that regard. We were all very close, Harry, Isabel, and I. She shared those things with us."

This time, Don and Shane exchanged glances. This likely confirmed the meeting with Glenn Weaver, which was what they wanted to establish. It also raised additional questions, but they did not need to know anything more concerning their investigation, at least not at this moment.

"Thank you, Mrs. Olson," Shane said. "I know that was very difficult and uncomfortable, but it's very helpful to our investigation. I think I'm done for now. Do you have any questions for us?"

Still sobbing, Elly said, "No, I don't think so. When can Harry come home so we can properly bury him?"

"Have you had time to decide on a funeral home?" Don asked. "If so, I believe the coroner can start things moving in that direction."

"The university has suggested we use Churchville Funeral Home here in town. They would like to do something special for Harry. Ethan McCallum told me that just this morning."

"Would you be okay if we asked the coroner's office to coordinate transport with Ethan?" Don Weston asked.

"Yes, Don. That would be a big help."

"Then that's what we'll do, and I'll ask Ethan to let you know when everything is arranged," Don said.

"Thank you, you've both been very helpful."

"Thank you, Mrs. Olson," said Shane. "You've also been very helpful."

THURSDAY

After Elly

After they left Elly, Don and Shane called Detective Rick Walker. "Rick," Shane said. "Can you meet us at Don's office? I want to review everything we know and don't know again. You've been with this throughout and may have something we've missed."

"Absolutely," said Rick. "I'll be there in ten minutes."

"Don, I'm still trusting you," said Shane. "What can you tell me?"

"On our last visit to the president's house, I pressed Elly for additional information in private. She confirmed a longstanding, intimate relationship with her and Isabel and the president. I hadn't told you because it hadn't come up before now; my apology."

"Apology accepted. I do trust your experience and judgment over mine or anyone else's in this investigation. Thanks for filling me in. I know you'll share more if needed."

It was 10:00 a.m. when they started a fresh pot of coffee. They went into a conference room, and Shane started writing on the dry-erase board. He put the names Harold Olson, Glenn Weaver, Isabel Helms, and James Giles at the top. "Stop me if I'm wrong at any point," Shane said. "Harold Olson. Deceased. Murdered by hanging. The body was found last Saturday afternoon. We have evidence of Glenn Weaver preparing the scene, a knife from Glenn Weaver's body that was used at the scene, and material from Glenn's home that appears to be consistent with a stun gun that might have been used on Harold Olson. All good so far?"

The other two men nodded. "If there were no other complicating factors, like our other cases, would we have been confident to charge Glenn Weaver with murder and believe we could win that case in a court of law?" Nodding heads. "Okay, let's consider that closed and move on to the next one."

"Wait," said Rick Walker. "Can we be sure the man in black is Glenn Weaver? Could it be James Giles? For that matter, the video is vague enough that it might not be a man. Could it be the missing Isabel, Elly Olson, or some other random killer?"

"Good points," said Don Weston. "We have no evidence of any kind that anyone was at the scene other than Harry and the shadow in black, but we do have video of Glenn's auditorium visits for several days. Strictly circumstantially, we could make an argument of premeditated preparation and make a case that Glenn Weaver is the only suspect who has the welding skill to secure the auditorium as we found it. He was not the only suspect with a possible motive, but I believe, independent of our other cases and outside of any new surprises, we would go to court with the video evidence and charge him with the murder of Dr. Olson."

More nodding heads. Don added, "There is also my regret that I knew Olson was missing the night before we found him. Had I been here, or returned immediately, would the outcome have been different?"

Shane commented, "Don, that's conjecture in hindsight. I could add a column for 'lessons learned,' but it doesn't change where we are today."

"Agreed," said Don.

"Let's move to Glenn Weaver," Shane said. "Also deceased. We are saying we believe he was the sole killer of Olson. After that murder, he went home and killed himself. He died from the effects of a fire that he set and left what would be considered a suicide note. We subsequently learned that he was dying from a fatal disease and knew it. We later discovered the terms of his separation from the university, which could speak to the motive for both the homicide and the suicide. From the autopsy, we also know there is an additional physical aberration that may have contributed to the behavior of Glenn Weaver, but there is no legal precedent for that condition as evidential. I'll note all of that here and under Olson as well. If we were dealing with this case on its own, I think we would all be comfortable labeling this death as a straightforward suicide. Correct?"

Rick spoke again, "We have no way of knowing that he was alone at the time of his death. The suicide note is typed and could have been placed there by anyone. I think we still have open ends, not likely ones, with other actors."

Don nodded. "More good points, and we have physical evidence to place James Giles at that scene at some point. We probably need more information from Giles at least."

"Noted," said Shane. "More thinking and information are needed before we slam the book on the suicide. Now the trifecta, Isabel Helms. Reported missing Monday, a week ago. Last Thursday, we discovered that we were missing her laptop. Since then, we have found she had a habit of meeting others anonymously and that included some BDSM elements. We know that from Glenn's Ironman correspondence, the wardrobe evidence at her home, and corroborating testimony from Mrs. Olson." He continued, making notes on the board, "We would consider her missing and presumed dead. We can't look at this one in isolation, based on the total circumstances and the discovery of her blood type on Glenn's knife. Based on the Ironman messages and the talk with Mrs. Olson, we think she met with Weaver on Friday, a week ago. Agreed?"

"Yes," said both men.

"Is it safe to assume from Glenn's note that there was at least one accomplice: 'I'll send a car for you'?"

"Yes," said both men again.

"We don't know where the meeting took place. It's likely at Glenn Weaver's residence, but we've found no trace of Isabel Helms' DNA or personal effects in sifting that entire crime scene. Her disappearance is still a mystery to be solved."

Shane continued, "So, we could say Glenn had the same motive here, as with Olson, but there are several things we don't know. Where did the meeting take place? Who was the accomplice or driver? Where is Isabel Helms and her laptop? Am I missing anything on this one?"

"That leaves James," said Don. Shane put a question mark under that name. He then wrote, "Accomplice? Driver?" Don continued, "We have some evidence that could place James Giles' car on Glenn's property at some point. Is he the James from the suicide note? James made the statement that Dr. Helms had abandoned her post at the school, and George Hunt let us know that James said Isabel had left town. It could be a useful hint, but it could also be idle gossip he picked up through the school grapevine."

"Giles seems to be our only real lead or connection right now," said Shane. "I wonder if we could get him to talk to us again."

"Probably not willingly," laughed Don. "But he's talking to an attorney now. Maybe his lawyer can help him figure things out."

FRIDAY

Vincent Reese

Vincent Reese had been in private practice for twenty-five years as a criminal attorney. He spent seven years before that as a state prosecutor. This wasn't the first time George Hunt had sent a client his way. This was the first time that George told him he believed strongly that the client had some involvement in the crime.

George also told him the client may be having some delusional issues that could be a contributing factor. Vincent was very aware of the case itself, as was anyone who kept up with the local news and gossip. The murder of a university president was an unprecedented, big deal for the small town. The complexity of other administrative and faculty deaths and a disappearance made it especially interesting from a legal perspective.

James Giles arrived at Vincent's office precisely at 9:00 a.m. He declined the offer of water or coffee and took a chair at the desk. Vincent thought he looked very small—not someone a jury would expect to be involved in violent crime. "Very nice to meet you, Dr. Giles," Vincent began. George Hunt had made sure he knew to call him 'Doctor.' "Where should we begin?"

"I'm not quite sure why I'm here at all. I've done nothing wrong."

"If George Hunt referred you here, his interest would be to make sure you are properly represented in a legal sense. He tells me you are being questioned by law enforcement. That doesn't mean you're a criminal, but if you have any involvement at all in what they are questioning you for, I need to know that to be of help. I understand from last night's news report that a suicide note referenced someone named James. Is that why you were being questioned by the police?"

"They told me about the note; I had no idea. I think they're trying to say I had something to do with Glenn Weaver's death."

"James—may I call you James?"

"Yes, that would be okay." It was one relational breakthrough.

"James, are you familiar with attorney-client privilege? I'm considering you a client now. It means that any confidential communications between the attorney and the client will remain secret. You can tell me anything. In fact, I need you to tell me everything if I'm going to represent you properly. Whatever you tell me stays between you and me, and I cannot be forced to disclose it. Do you understand that, and are you comfortable with it?"

"I know what it means."

"Good. Then, where should we begin? Perhaps you can tell me how you know Glenn Weaver."

"Glenn is an art instructor. As the academic dean of Churchville University, he is one of my faculty members." Vincent noted the present tense but made no comment.

"And what is the typical relationship between a dean and a faculty member?"

"The academic dean guides the university curriculum and the pedagogy of the faculty. He also decides which faculty members are academically worthy of tenure. Faculty members serve the university mission at the discretion of the dean and will follow his guidance."

"What was your relationship with Glenn Weaver as a faculty member?"

"Glenn Weaver is a visiting art professor. He was not on a tenure track, but I still monitor his work in the classroom and his scholarship. In his case, I would support his art exhibits."

"Support how?"

"I would visit gallery openings. The police say someone saw me with him at a show at YCCC shortly before his death. That somehow makes me a criminal to them."

"So, you have been in touch with him recently?"

"Yes, I did go to the YCCC show to support his art. When I visited with him, he told me the university had fired him."

"I would imagine that was disturbing to him?"

"He was very angry about it. He had no warning, and they just cut him off with no pay or benefits. He had terminal cancer, and they just cut him off."

"He told you he had terminal cancer?"

"Yes, he trusts me. No one else knew about it."

"Do we believe you are the James that he thanked in his suicide note?"

"I suppose I am. He trusted me and I supported him."

"How did you support him?"

"I stayed by his side all three nights of his art show, and we had dinner together."

"I need you to tell me whatever the two of you talked about. Did you think he was suicidal at that time?"

"Glenn told me he had made up his mind that he wouldn't treat the cancer. He really didn't have any choice anyway after the university fired him. He and I had both been mistreated by the current president."

"How were you mistreated?"

"I am the academic dean. The president made changes in the university that should not have been allowed without my approval. He changed my office without my approval, which is very disrespectful and wrong."

"What changes did he make?"

"He brought an old girlfriend to campus and made up a provost position for her. He changed the independent faculty disciplines to groups of confusion. He ruined everything we stood for and sent me away. I am currently on loan from the university to the Mennonite religious leadership to review their catechism. I should be returning to the office of the Academic Dean very soon to make corrections. The university has no leadership."

"Why do you believe the missing provost, Dr. Isabel Helms, I believe, was an old girlfriend?"

"Because everyone knew that Harold Olson was a skirt chaser and she followed him from his last school. And she's a prostitute."

"James, I'm going to get a bottle of water; can I bring you anything?"

"I would take a water, thank you."

Vincent took his time getting the water. When he returned, he didn't speak right away, pretending to check some messages. With his thoughts gathered, he began again. "James, what was your relationship with President Olson? You say everyone knew he was a skirt chaser. Did he make advances in that regard to anyone you knew?"

"No."

"Then, why would you say he was a skirt chaser?"

"Everyone knew. You could tell by the way he dressed and fixed his hair. He was always dapper. And he looked at pretty girls in a way that you knew."

"As the academic dean, would you have been privileged to know if any women had made complaints about him?"

"Certainly; the academic dean is the moral compass of the university."

"And there were no complaints that you were aware of?"

"There would have been; he had just gotten there at the time."

"So, 'everyone knew' was just a rumor at that time, but you believed there was some substance to it."

"It was obvious."

"Let's circle back to your relationship with the provost."

"I had none; she never asked for my advice. As the academic dean, I knew everything about the curriculum, the pedagogy, the faculty, and the way the university was supposed to work. I guess she thought she was smart enough to figure it out on her own. Either that, or she knew her boyfriend would take care of her no matter what she did."

"You said twice that she and Harold Olson had a personal relationship. Did you ever see or hear anything that specifically indicated such a thing?"

"Why else would a prostitute be the provost?"

"What makes you say she's a prostitute?"

"Glenn Weaver found that out when he checked her computer. He told me she had messages with men that she would meet."

"James, I want to make sure I'm not getting things confused here. Help me understand the circumstances where Glenn Weaver would be checking her computer and the subsequent discussion between you and Glenn. There must be some background before that."

"When I visited Glenn at the art show, we talked about how wrong things were at the university. I had been sent away so that the president and the provost could change everything without anyone to stop them. Now, they were firing faculty and going to make it a career school. The entire foundation and mission of the university were being destroyed by those two."

"So, you're telling me that the president and the provost were destroying the university, and no one but you would be able to stand up to them?"

"No one understood what was happening like I did, and no one had the power I had to stop it. I knew if we could prove who they were and expose their schemes, I could get rid of them and save Churchville University."

"So, that's why someone had to look into the provost's computer?"

"Yes."

"You and Glenn went to her office at the school?"

"No, she had an office at her house. She was smart enough that nothing was on her office computer. It was her personal computer that had all the filth."

"So, you went to her house and went through her computer. Was she there at the time?"

"I didn't go, but Glenn did. He said the house was not locked, so he just went in."

"Did he take her computer with him?"

"No, he didn't take anything. He's not a criminal."

There was a long pause. "James, technically entering her house and going through her personal belongings is a criminal act. Remember though, that under attorney-client privilege, I don't have to tell anyone what we discuss here. What did you and Glenn do with the information you found?"

"He went on her website and pretended he wanted to meet her. She had to wear a hood because it was a secret."

"And did they ever meet in person?"

"Yes, it was Friday, two weeks ago."

"And were you a part of that?"

"I drove her there, but I didn't stay."

"So, she knew you?"

"She was wearing a hood, so she wouldn't know anyone or where she was going."

"And where were you taking her?"

"To Glenn Weaver's barn."

"For what purpose?"

"I don't know. I thought he was going to take pictures that would prove the kind of woman she was. I didn't know anything else."

"Did you drive her back to her home?"

"He said she wouldn't need a ride. I left after I dropped her off."

RECAP WITH VINCENT REESE

" **J**ames, before I went into criminal defense, I was a state prosecutor. I tell you that because I think it gives me a two-sided look at evidence and testimony that can be an advantage for my clients. From what you've told me so far, in addition to what I know from public news coverage of the local murders, I completely understand why the police would want to talk to you."

"But I haven't done anything wrong. I've only tried to fix a wrong that was done to me and now done to poor Glenn Weaver. Harold Olson and Isabel Helms are the criminals. They've ruined people's lives and they're ruining the university. Their plans will hurt many more people. They must be stopped. They're sexual perverts and predators that can't be allowed to go unjudged."

"James, we must look at everything we discuss in the eyes of a judge and jury. Your defense and our legal plan depend on knowing that. Right now, the police are trying to solve a murder, an apparent suicide, and the whereabouts of a missing person. All are related by employment. We're a small town here, and this is probably the most sensational crime that has happened in the history of Churchville. We don't even have the resources to investigate it properly, so the state has had to come in to help. Knowing what you have just told me, if I were the state prosecutor, I would have you arrested now for knowledge of the breaking and entering."

"I've done nothing wrong," James said, agitated now.

"That would only be my first move, just to get you into further questioning. Charges from there could include accessory to murder, tampering with evidence, and possibly a case could be made for kidnapping."

"I don't know anything about any of that. All I've done is try to right a wrong in the eyes of God."

"James, would you be willing to talk to the police if I was there with you?"

"No, you've already told me what would happen. I'd be branded a murderer, and I've done nothing wrong."

"Okay, let's look at options. If they don't have any evidence other than what we know from the news, they probably can't charge you with anything. If they do have any evidence that we don't know about, you would likely be arrested and charged with something to hold you and brought in for further questioning. I would be with you, and I would not let you speak. I would expect that to happen soon."

"But I'm not a criminal."

"I believe I know exactly what you're thinking, James. I don't believe you're a bad person. I think we should give things a day or two. If they bring you in, I'll be there. If they don't, I'd advise you not to speak to anyone about any of this. Ever. If the police contact you for any reason, do not talk to them. Tell them that I am your attorney, and they have to talk to me. That's your right under the law. Understood?"

"Yes, I understand. You know I'm innocent."

"I know you wish for me to be your advocate on the grounds of your innocence. I also know the police and the state would like to find Isabel Helms and close this case. You know some things that would help with that, but you would also be implicating yourself as involved in some way. In your defense, I can't advise you to do that. Our best move is to do nothing and see what happens next. Do not talk to anyone about any of this and, if you are contacted by anyone, send them my way."

"Thank you," James said and left.

When James's car was out of the driveway and on the road, Vincent Reese called George Hunt, interrupting his chess game with Webster Hutchison. George answered his cell phone, "Vincent, what can I do for you?"

"Can you talk in private for a couple of minutes?"

"Yes, I think so. Webster, get lost. I need to talk to Vincent."

"Sorry to hear that," Webster laughed and left the room.

"All alone, Vincent. I trust this is about James Giles?"

"Yes; couldn't you think of someone else to send him to?"

George laughed. "Everyone deserves the best under the law. That left only you, of course."

"I'm glad you love me. Now, can you tell me what you know?"

"I believe I can, but it probably won't help. I cut him off when he told me he knew Glenn Weaver had entered Isabel's home uninvited and gone through her computer. I think it's safe to assume you already know that by now."

"I do. Is that all you know?"

"It was already more than I wanted to know."

"I understand."

"So, there is more?"

"Let's just say, I know why the police would want to talk to him. I've advised him to speak to no one and refer all requests to me."

"Well, that's always the right advice for a defense attorney. You can't go wrong there."

"We'll see what happens in the next couple of days. Just kidding about sending him to someone else; I always appreciate referrals, especially from you, George."

"I know the circumstances stink, but this is the kind of stuff that keeps us young."

"Thanks. I'll let you know how things turn out."

"Thanks, Vincent, I'd appreciate that."

FRIDAY

How to Talk to James

It was now almost noon. Chief Don Weston, Lieutenant Shane Mitchell, and Detective Rick Walker had been staring at the big question mark on the dry-erase board for some time.

Shane spoke first, "Last call. This is everything we know. Our two known crime scenes and Dr. Helms' house have no more evidence to offer. We're confident but still open to new evidence that Glenn Weaver killed Harold Olson and then committed suicide. We think now that Isabel Helms was killed earlier at the suicide scene, and we believe someone other than Glenn brought her to that scene, but we have zero hard evidence to prove that. We know James Giles was with Glenn Weaver shortly before this all started. We have a piece of evidence that places Giles at Weaver's home at some point, and we think Weaver acknowledged him in the suicide note. What do we have left?"

"Pretty much nothing," said Rick. "Without new information."

"And," Don said, continuing the thought. "We only know of one source to pursue for that information. That would be James Giles. We know he was set to talk to an attorney this morning. Should I call his lawyer to see how it went? I'm at a loss for any other direction to look in."

"Me too," said Shane.

Don called Vincent Reese. "Don, my friend. Good to hear your voice. I'd ask what you've been up to, but I think that's old news at this point."

"Getting very old, Vincent. I'm hoping you can make it new again."

"Probably not, but what's on your mind?"

"George Hunt called me yesterday. He had met with James Giles and said he was sending him your way this morning. Did that happen?"

"Yes, we spent about an hour together."

"Anything you'd be free to disclose."

"Sorry, Don," Vincent said. "There was nothing in our talk that was not in confidence. But, just talking from news reports, do you think it's at all possible that my client could have killed anyone?"

"Likely not, but, full disclosure, he appears to be our only source to fit pieces together in our missing-person puzzle. Do you think he would be willing to talk to us again?"

"I don't think so. I believe my client sees himself as the victim here. I've told him to speak to no one and refer any inquiries to me. Do you have anything you could charge him with?"

"Full disclosure again, maybe, but we don't think so. We do have some evidence that would be sufficient to bring him in for further questioning. I'd prefer to talk with him informally if possible."

"I've advised him against that, so I guess I'm no help at all," said Vincent.

"Not really," Don agreed. "But that's not your job. I am considering making a personal visit to him as an old friend to see if he would share anything at all that might help us."

"I get the sense that he's not considering you a friend at the moment, but there is nothing to stop you from visiting him. If he follows my advice, he'll send you back my way. If he doesn't, who knows?"

"I guess that's the way I'm looking at it."

"Will you let me know how it goes?"

"Absolutely. I expect he'll probably tell me to call you anyway. Well, Vincent, nice talking to you, as always. No doubt, we'll talk more as this continues. Thanks for your time."

"Thanks," said Vincent. "And good luck."

Vincent Reese thought about calling James Giles to let him know to expect a visitor, but he decided against it. Reese knew what Giles knew, and if his client chose to share it with Don, so be it. He'd done his required job with the legal advice he had already given.

"Well, gentlemen," Don said to Shane and Rick. "Does anyone have a better idea?"

"No," said Shane. "Trying to get Dr. Giles to talk is all we seem to have at this point, and your past relationship is our best hope for that."

"Okay," said Don. "Here's how I think we should do things. Let me know if either of you thinks otherwise. Rick, I'd like you to arrange for a uniformed officer from the county to go with me, someone professional but not physically intimidating. We can all go in Shane's unmarked car to meet them at the Sheriff's Office. I'll ride with the officer to James's house in their vehicle. If James discloses anything that would warrant an arrest, we'll be bringing him back with us. I'd like the two of you to follow us and keep a discrete distance at the house."

"I can do that," said Rick. "What are you expecting to happen?"

"Honestly, I don't know," replied Don. "James is not a stupid person. I guess I would expect that he'll tell the deputy and me to talk to his attorney and leave. Shane, what are your thoughts on this?"

"I think it's all we have to go on at this point, so let's do it and see where it goes," said Shane. "Having met Dr. Giles, I don't think we'll be well received. If he won't talk to us willingly, we have the vehicle evidence from the crime scene, and his attorney or one of our deputies will have to bring him in unwillingly. It would appear this is our last shot at taking the polite route. So, I'm good with the plan, but I think we should consider the timing. He just spoke with his attorney a few hours ago and left with the advice to not cooperate. I vote for letting him sleep on that advice and think over whatever he told Reese about a relationship with Glenn Weaver. There's no reason to rush this, and visiting him at a respectable hour tomorrow morning wouldn't hurt."

"Also," said Rick to Don. "I have a particular deputy in mind to join you. Not sure if she'd be available now, but we can easily line her up for tomorrow."

"Anyone I know?" asked Don.

"Deputy Melinda Parkinson?"

"Great call," said Don. "I do know her, and she's a perfect choice."

"So, our day is done," said Shane. "I think we should all go home and get a good night's rest. Don, as much as I love your company, I'm going back to Harrisburg tonight to sleep in my bed for a change. How about we all meet at the Sheriff's Office tomorrow morning at 10:00?"

The other two agreed.

SATURDAY

Last Call

Deputy Melinda Parkinson was already at the Sheriff's Office as Chief Don Weston arrived at 8:30. Melinda was a fifteen-year veteran of the Sheriff's Department. She'd lived in the local area forever. She had a liberal arts degree from Churchville University and a master's degree in Sociology. Her first career was several years of teaching high school in York. That's when she became convinced that her goal of participation in world peace could be better served in the calling to do police work. Her performance reviews would indicate that she made the right choice, and Melinda Parkinson was a great ambassador to the community.

"Good morning, Don," she said to the first arrival. "Good to see you again. I hear we're going perp hunting together." She laughed.

Don chuckled. "Probably more like we're off to get rejected by our prom date. Good to see you, too. This may or may not go anywhere, but when Rick told me you were his first choice, I wholeheartedly agreed."

"Must be a woman thing." She laughed again.

"You got me there. But it may also be a delicate, defusing thing, or nothing at all. I've seen you on campus in both of those roles, and you play them well."

She laughed again. "I have special expertise in the nothing at all category; that's always my favorite."

"Normally mine, too," said Don. "But I hope we'll get something more out of this one. Let's keep our fingers crossed."

Lieutenant Shane Mitchell and Detective Rick Walker trickled in at about 9:00 a.m. Melinda gave Don a thumbs-up as the other two men joined the conversation. "Morning all," said Shane. "What's so funny over here?"

Melinda responded, smiling, "Just the usual sexist and culturally inappropriate banter; you know how cops are. It's this or donuts."

Don said, "Melinda, please meet the esteemed Lieutenant Shane Mitchell from Harrisburg." They shook hands as Don continued, "Was it strange sleeping in your own bed last night?"

"Strange and very welcome," said Shane.

"Good, good," said Don. "Rick, do you have a conference room for us?"

"All arranged," said Rick. "I even have Melinda's favorite donuts."

"Let's do this," said Shane. "Don," said Shane as they walked to the room. "This one is your baby, so I want you to run the meeting and tell us what we need to do for you."

"Okay," Don said as they gathered coffee and donuts and got settled. "It's straightforward. Melinda and I will ride together in her cruiser and park in the driveway. Shane and Rick will take Rick's unmarked car and park on the street, a house or two down. You guys are just there in case we need witnesses for an arrest. I'm pretty sure Giles will send us away, so you're likely just along for a ride."

Rick spoke up, "Wasn't there a dog?"

"Glad you mentioned that; I completely forgot," Don replied. "It sounded like a big one. He put it in another room before he answered the door last time; hopefully, he'll do that again."

"Thought we should let Melinda know, just in case," said Rick.

"Good call; if it's like last time, we'll all know as soon as I ring the doorbell," Don laughed. "Any other thoughts from anyone before we head out?"

Melinda spoke this time, "So, I'll just follow your lead. If we're not making an arrest, I'll say and do nothing, right?"

"Right," said Don. And they headed to the cars.

On the way there, Shane remarked, "Rick, you know this really is our last shot. We can tie Isabel Helms to Glenn Weaver from email and the knife, but we can't prove a death or even a crime scene unless James Giles can tell us more."

"I know," said Rick. "I know."

Don and Melinda were quiet on the short drive. Don was thinking about how the last meeting with James had ended: "Don, you brought me here under false pretenses, and you should be ashamed of yourself. ... Do not contact me again." He hoped Giles would at least talk to him. Maybe his conscience, a couple of days and nights of thinking, and some guidance from George Hunt and Vincent Reese would soften his sting.

It was a beautiful, quiet Saturday morning when they pulled into the driveway and parked behind the Subaru wagon. Once again, as expected, the house erupted with wild barking when Don rang the doorbell. He could hear James Giles, but when he opened the door this time, a large, white German Shepherd sat at his side, obedient and alert.

"James," Don started. "This is Deputy Melinda Parkinson; she's just my ride to get here. I felt bad about how things ended on Thursday. You and I have a lot of years together, and I was hoping we could start over."

"I'm sure you know I shouldn't be talking to you," said James. "You need to leave and call my attorney if you have anything more to say."

"I know an attorney's advice would be not to speak with law enforcement," he acknowledged. "But, if you wanted to talk to a friend, I'd like to be a friend again."

James softened for just a second. Don wondered if there was a conscience there. Then, James stiffened and said, "Why should I ever trust you again?" Sampson was also on edge. "You lied to me," he said, his voice raised. "You said you needed help about the school, and you accused me of being a criminal—a murderer!" James was yelling now. The dog barked once, hyper-alert, sensing a threat.

"I'm sorry if it felt that way to you, James," said Don softly, hoping to inject some calm.

It was too late. James started to step forward. "Donald Weston, how dare you come here and try to trick me again! I've done nothing wrong, and I won't be treated like I have."

James took another step forward, and Deputy Melinda Parkinson instinctively stepped forward herself, putting an arm between James Giles and Don Weston. The giant dog, snapping, took Deputy Parkinson to the ground in one leap.

Then, there was a deafening explosion.

BANG

A 1911 Colt .45 is one of the loudest handguns on the planet. It is also devastatingly lethal, especially at close range. Sampson's head exploded in synch with the blast, and everything stopped, just for an instant.

Chief Don Weston went to the ground. He grabbed Deputy Melinda Parkinson by the shoulders. Knowing her hearing was affected by the firing of the gun, he looked her directly in the eyes and shouted into her face, "Melinda, are you okay?"

She shouted back, "Yes, yes; get this dog off me!"

Don holstered the .45. With his left hand, he effortlessly tossed the dead beast several feet away from Melinda. "Are you sure you are okay?"

"Yes," she said, struggling to her feet with Don's help. "I'm perfectly fine if a little deaf."

"That's good," said Don as Shane Mitchell and Rick Walker sprinted up to join the scene.

"Murderers!" screamed James Giles as he went to the dog's side. "Murderers! You will all burn in hell for your sins this day!"

At that moment, Don was no longer the polite, nice, gentle, small-town constable. He was in the 1980s, Philadelphia, street-cop mode as he responded angrily to James Giles, "There are worse places than hell and I'll be happy to introduce you to them very shortly. I'm going to take your advice to leave and call your attorney. You may wish to do the same. I will see the two of you in the interrogation room at the Sheriff's office in the next hour."

"Don't you dare threaten me!" yelled Giles. "I know my rights and I know my God and you can't order me around like that."

"You don't know shit!" Don yelled back in a booming voice that caused everyone, including Don, to fall silent. In the quiet seconds that followed, Don made a conscious break to de-escalate and compose himself before he spoke again. "Shane, Rick, Melinda, we're leaving now to go back to the sheriff's office. James Giles, you, and your attorney will meet us there in the next hour or I will personally return here to forcibly restrain you and deliver you there myself. That's not a threat; that's a promise." There was no more conversation and the law enforcement team left as a group.

Don had a private thought as he walked away from the scene. "Oh my God. Helen. I killed a dog."

"Don, I know you love dogs but they had it coming."

ATTORNEY-CLIENT RELATIONSHIPS

Not Always a Privilege

It was a silent ride in both cars heading back to the office. As they entered the building, Shane broke the ice, "Donuts and coffee, anyone?"

"I'll take my coffee as black as my murderous soul," said Don, rubbing his neck. All of them needed an intensity break.

Vincent Reese received two calls in quick succession. Dons was the first one. "Vincent, we're in a new ball game concerning your client, Dr. James Giles. We have direct evidence that places Giles at the scene of Glenn Weaver's death and the suspected scene of Isabel Helm's murder. I expect you to bring your client here within the next hour to answer our questions."

"Don," said Reese. "That certainly is a new wrinkle. I'll see what I can do."

"Your client has been informed that if the two of you can't make our invitation, I will personally detain him by less polite means and bring him here myself."

"Now, Don, you know he has rights that must be respected under the law."

"Vincent, so did Glenn Weaver and Isabel Helms. I know you better than this. This isn't the time for lawyer speak. It's the time to make you and James Giles present to hear our questions."

"I understand. I'll be there with Dr. Giles shortly."

"Thank you, Vincent."

Vincent's second call was, not surprisingly, from James Giles. Giles seemed to be crying as he blubbered out, "Attorney Reese, Police Chief Donald Weston has murdered my Sampson, and I want him to pay for it."

"Tell me what happened," responded Reese.

"A large group of police came to my private home and tried to make me talk to them. I told them they would have to speak to my attorney, and that they should leave the premises immediately. Sampson was protecting me. That's when they got upset and killed him. I was afraid they were planning to kill me, too. This whole thing needs to be stopped. The police must be made to pay for their violations." A loud sob, "They've harassed me and killed my only companion. I need you to uphold the law and take whatever action is needed for them to be punished for their wrongdoing."

"Dr. Giles, as your attorney, I am willing to accompany you to the Sheriff's Office and aid you in dealing with any charges that will put these cases to rest. Can you be ready shortly?"

After a pause for composure, Giles spoke "I'm ready now to do whatever it takes to put an end to this police action. I have extremely important work to do at the university, and I won't put up with these interruptions any further."

"I'll be on my way to the Sheriff's Office in fifteen minutes," said Reese. "Can you meet me there?"

"Yes."

As he hung up the phone, Vincent Reese thought, "That was easy."

INTERROGATION

Attorney Vincent Reese waited in the parking lot of the Sheriff's Office for the arrival of James Giles. Reese didn't know what to expect once they entered the building, but he knew the police had sound cause for this visit. He knew his client had information that would benefit their investigation.

When James arrived, he was still agitated over the recent incident with the dog. He was overly talkative about his persecution as well. Reese told him, "I know you're upset and angry, and feeling very hurt and wronged. I know we're here to take steps that will resolve those issues for you, but I don't know for sure what will happen when we go inside. Remember that I am here to represent you. If you have been completely honest with me, I think you'll be okay. You don't have to say anything, and you can ask me if you want guidance, but I won't stop you if you need to talk."

Lieutenant Shane Michell and Detective Rick Walker met Reese and Giles at the door and escorted them to the interrogation room. "Why are we going in here?" asked Dr. Giles. "I'm here to file a complaint."

"We'll get to that soon," said Reese. "Let's get this out of the way first."

The four men, Reese, Giles, Mitchell, and Wilson, were the only attendees. Don, Deputy Melinda Parkinson, and Sheriff Bill Hester were on the other side of the glass. Shane opened, "Mr. Reese, Dr. Giles, thank you for joining us. As you know, there have been several incidents of concern surrounding the Churchville University campus. We have a confirmed murder of Dr. Harold Olson, a presumed suicide of Glenn Weaver, and a missing person case of Dr.

Isabel Helms. We believe these are all related events. We also believe that you, Dr. James Giles, may have some additional information that can help us in these matters."

"Do you think I murdered Dr. Olson?" asked Giles in a raised voice, "Like you murdered my Sampson.".

"Dr. Giles," said Reese. "You don't have to say anything here."

Mitchell continued, "No, Dr. Giles. No one believes you murdered President Olson, and there is no evidence of that. Does that help?"

Silence.

"There is," said Shane, setting the bag with the broken lens on the table, "evidence that your vehicle was at the residence of Glenn Weaver. We know he died there, and we believe that the same site is a crime scene related to our missing person, Dr. Isabel Helms. We found this lens there. We also confirmed you had such a repair done to your vehicle the Monday after Glenn Weaver's death. Would you care to help us understand why you were there?

Giles was quiet at first, but then he jumped to his feet and shouted, "God damn it! God damn it! God damn it! That Glenn Weaver messed everything up!"

"How so?" questioned Shane, looking directly at Vincent Reese, expecting an objection.

Reese didn't stop James Giles; instead, he turned to Dr. Giles and said, "James, have a seat. Do you want to tell them anything more?"

James Giles hesitated. A line had been crossed. He then sat down and sputtered in anger, "Glenn was supposed to expose and embarrass the president and the provost, nothing more. They were evil, but I didn't know he would kill anyone!"

"How were they evil?" asked Shane.

"He was a womanizer, and she was his prostitute mistress. They destroyed the academic stature of Churchville University. They were evil, and God knew it."

"Do you have first-hand knowledge of an affair between the two administrators?" Shane asked, running with the rant.

"Glenn found everything on Dr. Helms' personal computer. He looked it up at her house when she was away. She was a prostitute."

Rick joined the party. "Dr. Giles, we know that Glenn Weaver had correspondence with Isabel Helms about a 'dungeon.' Were you aware of that?" There was no interjection from Reese.

"She was always having sex with men she didn't even know. She was an un-Godly woman. I don't know anything about a 'dungeon.' I took her to Glenn's barn."

"You took her?" said Rick.

"Yes, that's when my taillight got broken. That road is a mess."

"What happened when you took her there?"

"I don't know. Glenn was supposed to take pictures of her that would show the world what she was. He told me she didn't need a ride home and I left."

"What were your thoughts when you heard she was missing?"

"I didn't think a thing. I didn't care. I was only glad she was no longer provost. Once we exposed Dr. Olson as a fraud for all his marital affairs against God's wedding vows, I could go back to the dean's position. The school needs my direction to be saved."

"What were your plans for Dr. Olson?"

"I wanted the world to know he wasn't a good man so the board of the school could send him away like the last charlatan president. Glenn said he could take care of that."

"What did you expect he would do?"

"I didn't know, but he called me Saturday evening. He said he was on his way home to retire for good. I could tell he was already hopped up on drinking or drugs or something. He told me the president was as gone as the provost and said I'd hear it on the news. I went straight to his house. God, he messed everything up!

"He was in the barn on the floor, stoned out of his mind. The place was already starting to burn and full of smoke. I left the door open. The smoke cleared some and I tried to talk to him. He was just stupid. I asked him what he had done. He just laughed. He pulled a knife out of his pocket and handed it to me. 'Have a souvenir,' he said, and he just kept giggling. God told me what to do next and I plunged the knife into his heart to send his evil spirit to hell. I wiped off the knife handle and walked away, closing the door to hell behind me."

Everyone hit pause at the enormity of this unexpected news. "There, I said it; I killed Glenn Weaver, but he killed everyone else and had to die for his sins."

Reese said to the room, "I think we're done here for now."

"Agreed," said Shane. "Rick, would you show Dr. Giles and his attorney to the holding cell? I believe they'll want to have some further conversation in private."

Don, Melinda, and Sheriff Hester joined Shane in the interrogation room. "Good job," laughed Don. "You even got him to confess to a murder he didn't commit."

"Good job, everyone," he continued. "Everything should wrap up pretty quickly from here and we can all get some rest."

NOT SO FAST

"**W**ork's not over," said Sheriff Bill Hester. "I can't hold James Giles here unless he's charged with a crime and formally arrested. Do we have charges?"

Deputy Melinda Parkinson spoke first, "I think he's an accessory to murder. He brought Isabel Helms to Glenn Weaver to be killed."

Shane said, "What murder? We have no evidence of murder without a body or Glenn's corroboration, which is unlikely at this point."

"We have her blood on the knife," said Deputy Parkinson.

"True," said Shane. "But playing devil's advocate, the knife could have been taken from her home. She could have cut herself cutting vegetables. We know she's missing, but we have no proof that she's been murdered. We also have no evidence that James Giles had any involvement with the death of Dr. Olson."

"So, he just gets away with everything?" asked Melinda.

"I don't think so," offered Chief Don Weston. "The rest of the blood evidence and Giles' own words convict him. We know he didn't kill Weaver, but his description of the stabbing, his action, and intent, is the textbook definition of attempted murder."

As all parties let that sink in, Rick spoke, "We have no evidence to place Giles anywhere at the Helms house or the auditorium scene. It's not a crime for him to have dinner and conversation with Weaver. Hard evidence places his car at Weaver's property but doesn't define that he was there or if he was present for any crime. The only serious criminal charge we have would be based on his admission of intent to murder when he stabbed Weaver."

"Again, Shane," said Don. "Good job on getting him to confess to a murder he didn't commit." Don turned to Hester. "Bill, your thoughts?"

"I think that's the correct option. Dr. Giles didn't kill anyone, Weaver did. None of us believe Giles is without involvement in the overall picture of the murder of the missing provost, but there is no evidence to charge him in those actual activities. The only real charge I see is in his own, damning admission of killing Weaver, whether he did or not."

Shane closed the meeting, "Next step, in the presence of his defense attorney, Detective Walker and I will officially charge and arrest Dr. James Giles for the attempted murder of Glenn Weaver. All in agreement?"

All heads nodded.

THE AFTERMATH

Churchville University had an impressive funeral mass and procession for their fallen president, Dr. Harold Olson. WYCC, hosted by Alvin Corson, covered the entire service for their audience. The new library was named for Dr. Olson in honor of his leadership and tenure. The Dr. Harold Olson Learning Center would be his perpetual legacy.

Elly Olson moved back north. She and the kids, Harold Jr. and Cindy, were taking a long vacation to Australia this year. The Crocodile Hunter Zoo had been on Harry Sr.'s bucket list. Harry Jr. had a crush on Bindi Irwin and hoped to meet her.

Don called his old friend Darell Metz.

"Still pissing on your dumpster fire?" answered Darell with a laugh.

"Stubbornly but finally extinguished," said Don reflectively. "Just rummaging through some cold ashes now."

"All missing persons accounted for?"

"Actually, no. George Olson is dead. He was tortured, emasculated, and killed. Our missing faculty member indeed committed suicide by fire, as we suspected at the time. So, we found those two."

"Who killed Olson?"

"Suicide guy. Turns out he had a recent terminal cancer diagnosis. In cost-cutting measures at the school, he had been fired. With no severance and little time left, he probably felt he had nothing more to lose."

"Wow, and the provost?"

"Never found a trace of a body. We think suicide guy killed her. He had been stalking her online."

"I'm confused."

"We were too. A clue from the suicide note led us to an accomplice who eventually cracked."

"Really?"

"Really, it was the former dean who had been replaced by the provost."

"There's a new twist I hadn't heard." Darell laughed again. "Now I'm sorry I missed all the fun."

"I haven't even told you about the fun part yet," said Don. "The president and his wife and the provost had been involved in a love triangle for years, and the provost had a BDSM fetish. You should have seen her wardrobe."

"Yikes, I guess our cop sense was still in working order. Too bad we couldn't have followed that one further in our search. I hope you saved some slinky lingerie for me. I'm partial to fishnet stockings, you know." More laughter.

"I didn't know that for sure but I'll keep it in mind. As if I could ever erase the mental image."

"Any other juicy tidbits?"

"Too many to tell. Sadly, I even killed a dog. We'll spend a day or more on it with your next visit. I'll drive you around to the scenes of the crimes. You'll love it."

"I'm planning my trip now."

"Give me a few weeks. I have another trip planned with the former university president, another old friend."

"So, two dead, one still missing, presumed dead, what happens to your remaining accomplice?"

"Another small twist I'll fill you in on later, but he's been charged with the attempted murder of suicide guy. No doubt an attorney will get that reduced to second-degree aggravated assault. Our former dean will remain in custody until he begins his likely five-year sentence in the York County Prison. This guy's not built for prison, so he should have an enlightening time there."

"No doubt. You might get him some lingerie as well. Stay dry, I'll be up your way before you know it."

"Thanks, Darell, looking forward to your company, as always."

George Hunt and Don Weston took the promised trip to Gettysburg.

EPILOGUE

Gettysburg

Don Weston and George Hunt were just an average pair of amateur Civil War historians taking a drive to the mecca of their common interest.

Don was filling George in on some of the choices for the outing, "George, you know my ex-cop group of Civil War buffs and reenactors does an annual big trip up here. We rent an old farmhouse through VRBO that puts us in the middle of everything by day and the middle of nothing by night. It's really been the perfect period-correct get-away. Fortunately, it was available for us for a couple of days between long rentals. You're going to love our lodging."

"Don, I think I'd love anything right now that is not Churchville. I didn't have half the involvement you had in the recent history there, but I had enough to want to get away to history anywhere else. I was glad you asked me to escape with you, and I'd be happy if we were staying in pup tents."

"I wish I'd know that," said Don. "I went ahead and rented an 1800s farmhouse on forty acres. I probably could have saved a couple of bucks."

After a great meal, the two men settled into the night in comfortable rocking chairs with their cigars and after-dinner drinks. The porch was lit only by a couple of kerosene lanterns on sconces attached to the pillars. A period-correct calm surrounded the house with the soft light and the fireflies. George broke it with one of the elephants in the room.

"Why did you have against the dog, Don?"

Don laughed out loud. "The dog had the deputy on the ground and was at her throat. 'Down boy' didn't seem to be nearly as effective in saving her."

"Just kidding," George chuckled. "I couldn't resist. A new school year," said George. "A fresh start. With the faculty changes in the last administration and an incoming freshman crop, we get about twenty-five percent turnover in our little community. The events of last year will be quickly lost to time. What are your plans for the coming year?"

Don took a long drag on the Punch and slowly responded through a cloud of smoke, "I've been thinking about retiring from the school. I've got plenty of law enforcement consulting work to keep me going. Last semester reminded me of why I took my first retirement from Philadelphia."

"I'd hate to see you go right now."

"We can still do this," said Don. "I wouldn't be leaving town, just leaving Churchville University."

"The reason I'd miss you," George said, "is I'm going back to Churchville."

"No shit," said Don, surprised.

"None at all," said George. "You're the first person outside of the Board of Directors to know."

"I guess that's a privilege," said Don. "How did this come about?"

"The Board contacted me shortly after the last president was gone. In truth, they never wanted me to retire the first time, and they made that clear. They also knew I was working closely with the past administration and wanted me to continue things on that path. Honestly, I've been a little bored at the law office, and now that the university is trying to take on some of the challenges they wouldn't take seriously in the past, I think I'd enjoy the new test. Would my returning help change your mind about staying?"

"I think that could change a lot of things in a good way," said Don in another cloud of smoke. "But there's more on my mind, so let's hold the closing statement for some time after tonight."

"Understood," said George. "I shall consider the rest of our time together as a recruiting trip."

"Then, I can expect the university will pick up our dinner bill tomorrow? I'm pretty sure with appetizers, dessert, and a bottle of wine or two, I can get us over the $300 mark at Dutch's Daughter." Don laughed.

After hiking the battlefield the next day and driving the surrounding countryside, they arrived at Dutch's Daughter for an early dinner at 4:30 and didn't leave until 7:00. As promised, Don ate and drank the bill up to $307.82. George dropped an $80 tip on top of that, satisfied that he'd get the return he was hoping for. By 8:30, they were back on the porch with the kerosene lamps and fireflies.

BACK AT CHURCHVILLE

Chief Don Weston was back for the new semester. George Hunt had sealed the deal with another excessive dinner at The Paddock on Market in York. The way to a man's heart.

Lying in bed that night, Don said out loud, "I love you, Helen, thanks for everything."

ACKNOWLEDGMENTS

Thank you for reading 'Final Exam'. If you are new to my writing, I welcome you. If you came here by way of 'Blame it on the Moon,' I welcome you back! Either way, I'd greatly appreciate it if you could find the time to submit a review of your thoughts on the book, whether you loved it or not. One of the best things about this writing journey is connecting with readers. I love to visit the classrooms, book clubs, writer's groups, etc. that give me the confirmation and/or direction to continually improve in this craft. If I can't meet you in person, you can still connect with me directly through my web site loupuglieseauthor.com. I read and respond to those notes personally and will continue to do so as long as I can.

My continued thanks always to my wife, Kathy, and our dog, Mitch. They remain by my side for every bit of this journey. It's their permission, support, and encouragement that allows me to sit at the laptop and smoke cigars for the many hours and days and months it takes for the inspirations and research to become something for a reader to enjoy.

My Mom has been gone since 1989 but she was always the largest influence in my education, career, and writing. She and my late Father and the rest of the family still give me guidance, if only in my mind.

On the professional side, I've had a wonderful opportunity over the past several years to learn from The Florida Writers Association (FWA) and the Mystery Writers of America (MWA). Thanks to my FWA mentor, Vic DiGenti, I've been blessed with hosting a monthly chapter of that organization, allowing me to regularly meet new writing contacts like Shutta Crum, my Alpha beta reader for 'Final

Exam.' I also continue to learn how to judge writing, especially my own, from Elaine Senecal and the Royal Palm staff.

Other authors, from novices like myself to New York Times Bestsellers like Lisa Black, have been extremely generous with their time and patience. It's a fascinating world of creative minds. I feel like I'm still an intern in this craft but so many of them have welcomed me and encouraged me and treated me as a peer. It's an amazing community of 'Writers Helping Writers' out there.

The book construction and assembly team from 'Blame it on the Moon', returned for 'Final Exam' and I hope to work with them on the next sequel and many other works to come. That would be Editor Jennifer Ellen Cook. cover designer, Christine Holmes, and formatter, Autumn Skye. I'd never be able to competently stumble my way through publication without them.

Thanks again for your time and interest in my work. I now return to the writing chair on the pool deck with my dog and cigars. The Vicki Roadcap sequel to 'Blame it on the Moon' is coming next!